Dick Cheney shot me in the face*

Dick Cheney shot me in the face*

*And other tales of men in pain
by **Tim O'Leary**

RARE BIRD
LOS ANGELES, CALIF.

THIS IS A GENUINE RARE BIRD BOOK

Rare Bird Books
6044 North Figueroa Street
Los Angeles, California 90042
rarebirdbooks.com

For more information, address:
Rare Bird Books Subsidiary Rights Department
6044 North Figueroa Street
Los Angeles, California 90042

Set in Minion
Printed in the United States

10 9 8 7 6 5 4 3 2 1

Library of Congress data available upon request.

My thanks to Monica, Claire, Bonnie Jo, Steve, Jack, Jill, Jeff, and the Portland Writer's Group for their help in crafting these stories.

And of course, to Michelle.

CONTENTS

DICK CHENEY SHOT ME
IN THE FACE

I WAS CROUCHED HALF-MAST, watching my bird-dog Belle nudge a sharp-tail out of a patch of buffalo grass, when Dick Cheney shot me in the face. If you know anything about shotguns, the fact I'm alive to tell this story borders on a miracle. Lucky for me, the Vice President was shooting small—an ancient 20-gauge packed with bird shot—supposedly a gun Gerald Ford gave Dick in 1974 for running his presidential campaign.

Jesus, if I have to hear that story one more time.

If he'd been using a grownup's gun, a 12 or 16-gauge, it would've been closed-coffin. At the very least, I'd be sucking dinner through a straw while watching cartoons from a chrome wheelchair. Fortunately, the Vice President couldn't hit a barn door from thirty feet. He favors himself quite the sportsman, but after hunting and fishing with the guy for thirty years, I can tell you there's a lot of legend in Cheney Ville. Fact is, Dick rattles easy. When those wings whistle and a grouse goes vertical, he does a little Halliburton two-step, prancing around like he just got to invade another Arab nation. A man that understands hunting plants himself, calmly leading the bird.

Ironically, his shitty hunting skills saved my life. I only took the tail-end of the load; though to this day I've no clue what he was shooting at. What I can say, is that getting shot in the face is a life-changing experience. I'd turned my head a touch when I heard the blast, and next thing I know I'm lifted off my feet and tipped over, pellets burrowing a quarter inch into my face and neck like big iron ticks.

The scalp is a big bleeder, and when there's that much blood you can't tell how hurt you are. I mean, nick your leg with a chainsaw and you can at least see if it's still attached, but good luck figuring out a head wound. I lay there, wondering if this was it. One eye blind with blood, the one I lost that day. Through the other I could see him bent at the waist, staring down on me, even whiter than normal. Corpse white. That artificial ticker maybe not pumping all the way to his brain. The sun at his back, his sweaty bald head and glasses reflecting light, there was this eerie halo around him, like some kind of warped angel. I thought, "If I'm dead and Cheney's here, something's gone terribly, terribly wrong."

"Henry? For God's sake Henry, are you alright?"

And that was the last time I ever saw Dick Cheney.

Two Secret Service guys, Lurch and Larry, I liked to call them, whisk him away before I can even raise my head an inch. You'd have thought it was Dick that'd been shot, men yelling into their sleeves, "Angler out, Angler out." Angler, his code name. Jesus, we don't have anglers in the West; we have fishermen. But Dick has to be all Isaac Walton, or act like a British lord making a big ta-do. Cheney, man of the land, slayer of fish. Hell, when he casts a fly it's more apt to end up in the back of someone's head than a rainbow's mouth. If Dick's in the boat, de-barb those hooks and duck for cover!

Big black Escalades tore through my field, and like magic, men surrounded Dick, shoving him like a sleeping bag head-first into the back. And me? I'm left lying in the dirt, blood piddling down my face, Belle whimpering as she circles me. I reached up to feel the lead pellets lodged in my skull before holding out a limp hand to comfort her, Belle sniffing hard to see if she smelled death.

Finally, a couple more of the big boys hoisted me up and laid me flat in the back of a four-wheeler, me yelling, "Don't forget Belle," and off we went, bouncing up and down on hard carpet, tearing up even more of my wheat. I smelled iron, unsure if it was blood or just the normal odor of a government rig; the pungent bouquet of bullshit. Once we hit the highway, they lit up the siren, and it's off to the hospital in Jackson Hole. Shock and awe all the way, everything on the road pulling to the side, this being one instance when I appreciated executive power.

For the next hour, they tweezed pellets out of my noggin and neck. Cleaned out my eye socket to someday fit me with a glass peeper. When I awoke, my wife Cindy was bedside, angry and worried, rocking in her seat, fists balled as if she's preparing to mount a horse that doesn't particularly want to be ridden.

"I told you not to go. Man's a menace. But no, you're a big shot. Hunting with the Vice President. Big goddamn deal. See what that gets you? Your head almost blown off, and damn near blind."

Cindy-speak for, "Oh my God, how are you feeling?" And I'm thinking, *It's a good thing Dick didn't kill me, because Cindy would've beaten him to death with that leather-strapped sawed-off pool cue she keeps under the front car seat.* "Just in case I run into someone lacking manners," is how she explains the weapon.

A few minutes later, some other pencil-neck crept into my room. I'd seen him a couple times hovering around Dick. Pure Washington, but "westernized" in a leather vest and shiny black shit-kickers.

"Mr. Thomas," he said, and shakes his head with fake concern. "I'm Lawrence Hovey, I work for the Vice President. How are you? I'm so happy to see you awake and looking so good under the circumstances." He smiled like a man that just farted and plans to blame the dog.

I eyed him, with what was left of me, and grunted. "Where's Dick?"

"The Vice President was called back to Washington, an emergency. He wanted me to check in on you, make sure you're comfortable and have everything you need. We did some background on the surgeon here, a real top-notch fellow, as good as you could get anywhere in the country."

I didn't mention what little comfort that was for a man with an empty crater in his head. Instead, I pondered myself with an eye patch, like Lee Marvin in Cat Ballou.

"So, Mr. Thomas, as you can imagine, this is a pretty sensitive situation. The press and all. If they get wind of a hunting accident, they'll have a field day. The Vice President has to deal with them on a daily basis. The personal intrusions, the insults, all part of his job. But you certainly didn't sign up for that, did you? It's important we have a discussion on the best way to handle this. You know, to protect you and your family. The press can be very disruptive."

Cindy poked at him with her long index finger, the "finger of truth" I call it, with the power to cut through bullshit. "Disruptive?" she yelled. "Know what's disruptive? Being blind! Walking around with a white cane and a dog to lead you to the bathroom. Making your living with a tin cup and a dancing monkey as your partner. That's disruptive."

I appreciated Cindy's flair for drama, but clearly I was only half blind and didn't require any assistance from an animal. Turning toward Hovey, I said, "You don't need to worry, I'm not talking to the press." Which sounded like "Snudan'tned to voory," my lips still rubbery from the anesthesia.

Truth is, if I wanted to tattle on Dick Cheney, I'd have a lot more to talk about than his lack of field-sport skills. Dick and I, we'd been acquainted most of my life. We met at Natrona High School in Casper in the fifties. I wouldn't say we were friends, but we shared a love of beer, which sometimes brings men together. After we graduated, the government offered me a vacation abroad, all expenses paid, as in "C'mon kid, see the world, or at least Vietnam." Dick, well, he had a real aversion to uniforms, racked up five deferments, and became one of the most legendary draft dodgers in Wyoming history.

I went off to Texas for boot camp and then shipped overseas; first time I'd ever been outside of Wyoming. I didn't follow politics much; at that age it was all ice-cold brew and girls. I just knew my Dad and

Granddad had served their time in the big wars, and if the country needed me it was my duty to show up. Most of us in Wyoming felt that way, which is why I couldn't figure Dick out.

The Army tended to regard country boys as pack mules, assigning us jobs we'd be doing at home, primarily walking across fields shooting at stuff. But in Vietnam, stuff tended to shoot back, which kind of changed the whole experience. There were a lot of adjustments. In Wyoming it might hit 100 degrees, but never with 100 percent humidity, and you don't have seven-foot long snakes that can swallow a good-sized dog. Or little kids that will accept a Hershey bar with one hand and shoot your nuts off with the other.

I did, however, learn a few useful skills. I can rig a bicycle seat with a tiny bit of C4 so it blows your ass thirty-feet skyward. I got real good at stuffing a grenade down a rabbit hole while running full-tilt. My marksmanship improved. I can pretty much plant one dead center in the brain bucket from two hundred yards. Or at least I could until Cheney shot out my sighting eye.

Of course, I gave up defending the war. When I got out and took the time to educate myself about the political hi-jinx and economic motivations, I developed a different perspective. But I'm proud of those of us that did the job. The army—the working grunts—ain't about politics. It's about following orders, getting done what needs to be done, and if you're lucky, surviving.

Cheney managed to avoid the good and bad of that life experience. Instead of boot camp, he opted for Yale, where he promptly flunked out. Twice. I guarantee it wasn't due to lack of brain power. Like him or not, Dick's one of the smartest men I ever met. My guess is that he just thought he knew better than all those professors.

I ran into him when I was home on leave, Dick occupying himself by trying to talk another college into keeping him out of harm's way. We ended up hoisting a few, Dick real curious about military life and full of questions about Nam. He decided it was about the last place he wanted to be, and if the military came breathing down his neck, he'd join the Coast Guard.

"The Coast Guard? Dick, you've never been near a body of water you couldn't swim across while holding a can of Bud. What the hell do you know about boats and the ocean?"

"All I need to know is that any coast I'd be guarding would be seven thousand miles from Vietnam. Hell, maybe they'll put me down south, protecting Malibu Beach. Keep watch over all those girls in bikinis. Maybe I'd even meet that cute little Annette Funicello. Play a little beach blanket bingo. I've always wanted to spend some time with that little Mouseketeer. I think that's the kind of duty I might enjoy." Dick has a way of saying things, no matter how stupid, with such confidence that you want to believe him.

We were in his Dad's pickup, three sheets to the wind, headed to our fourth watering hole when Dick drove into a ditch, taking out twenty feet of fence and awarding him the first of his two DUIs. Me? I ended up in the hospital, ten stitches in my forehead. It occurs to me now that the scars on my face are a map of Cheney's screw-ups.

I lost track of him for quite a few years, and next thing I heard he's a big shot in Washington, first working for some Congressman, and then as an assistant to President Ford. Pretty amazing to everyone who knew him back home. We all figured it must not be that tough to become a success in Washington.

After my honorable discharge, I married Cindy, who'd always been the one and only for me, and we worked my dad's spread until he died. Then we sold his tired place, moved to Jackson Hole, and managed to buy a lot of land in the valley when it was just another nothing Wyoming town. Twenty years later the Richie Riches start moving in, building fake multi-million dollar ranches and hunting lodges. At first, most of them were oil men that would visit now and then to see their money bubble out of the ground, treating Wyoming like their own little Saudi Arabia. Then the Hollywood-types showed up. They could hide on a thousand acres, still find a good steak, and there was no income tax. "C'mon out to the ranch and we'll go fly fishing or skiing," they'd say to their fancy friends.

During tourist season the streets filled with citidiots buying two hundred dollar Stetsons and silver-tipped Tony Llamas. Suddenly I'm selling ground to these knuckleheads for fifty, even a hundred times what I paid for it, and I wake up one day an average guy with a good bit of coin. Until then, our biggest dream had been to make the bank payments, and maybe have enough left over to drive to Denver every couple years to see the Broncos play. This "rich" thing was a total surprise.

And that's about the time I hooked up again with Cheney. He was running for Congress, comes to Jackson Hole for a fundraiser, and of course, hits me up for a donation. Then Dick wants to shoot birds or an elk, maybe bring some of his big donors out to "his good friend Henry's spread" to catch some cutthroat. Make him appear a man of the land. A real American.

As usual, Cindy called it right. I fell for it. Mr. Big Shot. Pretend friends with Cheney. I admit I loved going into town and have the boys ask, "How's your buddy the Congressman?" I'm not the kind of guy who would ever ask for anything, but somehow it made me feel important just knowing I could. Not proud of that, but it's a fact.

To make it worse, Cheney kept working his way through Washington like a nasty strain of the flu. Next thing you know, he's the Secretary of Defense. Right, the guy who avoided the Army like a grungy toilet seat. The way I see it, if you're put in charge of sending men to war, you ought to damn well have been there yourself, seen firsthand what human carnage looks like up close. Taking in a Rambo flick won't do.

After that he's a Bush fixture, so we weren't surprised when he got named Vice President under Junior. Once a year or so, I'd get the call: "Vice President Cheney is scheduled in Jackson, and he'd like to come out to your place," more an order than a request.

It had nothing to do with friendship. We never engaged in heartfelt conversations, just two guys getting older discussing all they'd learned. No deep thinking from Dick, who tended to focus on his own paranoia, infused with a lot of hate. Cheney was like a turn-of-the-century aristocrat, Baron Baldy Von Uptight. Dick and his old white men cronies lived in a different century, while the rest of the world moved on. Though we were waving the same flag, his America looked a lot different than mine.

But I wasn't about to tell that story, that we were really just using each other. I have no desire to be seen wearing an eye patch in People Magazine or sitting across from Larry King. OK, I might like to sit with that Katie Couric. She's got some firecracker in her. But no interest in the press. Not my style.

In other words, I never said a thing.

And guess who else never said a thing? Dick Cheney. You might've thought he'd call and apologize. Send over a nice bottle of scotch with a card, "Sorry I can't shoot straight, keep an eye out for me." Hell, I'd have laughed over that.

Then about a year later I saw he did it again. Apparently too embarrassed to hunt in Wyoming, Dick travelled to Texas and shot someone else in the face. Naturally, I'm interested. Dick's hunting with an old fellow named Harry Whittington, and it's pretty much a repeat performance, only way rougher for Harry. He's also hit in the chest, and while he's in the hospital has a heart attack and a lung collapses. Harry took a bigger load, around 200 pellets, and to this day some of the metal is still inside him, too close to vitals to yank out. Your body has a way of cleaning itself up, sometimes working shrapnel to the surface. I think about poor Harry, sitting at breakfast, when he feels a BB bubble-up, a bloody little thing popping out of his chest and into his oatmeal while he sips his coffee, just to remind him of Dick.

The sad thing? Harry barely knew Cheney. He'd donated a few bucks, was asked to go hunting, and next thing he's in the hospital while they're putting paddles to him. Then the press converges, hounding him for weeks. Cheney's people made a half-assed attempt to blame Harry, as if he was stupid enough to jump in front of a man firing a shotgun. From what I could tell, Harry's the genuine deal, not saying much, not blaming anyone. Just acting the southern gentleman. There was one thing that particularly caught my attention. When the press asked him if Dick ever apologized, Harry just smiled and changed the subject.

And I couldn't help but feel guilty. If I'd come forward when Dick shot me, maybe Harry would've thought twice about going hunting with the guy. The idea haunted me, until I just decided we had to talk, one Cheney survivor to another. So, I called down to his law office in Austin. It was tough to get through. I'm sure he's tired of people bringing up the subject, so I left him a voice mail. A couple days later, he called back, and I could tell he was skeptical, but we talked, and after a while got comfortable, discovering we've got more in common than being Cheney survivors. Harry seemed the kind of man I'd appreciate sitting down and having a drink with, his head screwed on straight. Certainly a conservative type, but we share the belief that America also stands for a level playing field. It didn't devolve into a Cheney bitch session, but it did occur to us that hanging around with him was risky to our health, and maybe dangerous for other reasons too. When you stand behind a man, people naturally assume you also stand for him, and I suspect we both saw a different America than Dick.

We discussed living on the land, driving down dirt roads, thinking how wonderful it was that God put us in such a place. And here's what you learn when you live in the country. Part of being a good neighbor is warning people about dangerous situations, and yes, keeping an eye out for each other. When I'm driving and come across a herd of elk crossing the road, or see a patch of black ice, I flash my lights to warn oncoming cars. Give them a head's up. When my neighbors are safe, I'm safe.

FIRST KILL

ON FRIDAY NIGHT JUSTIN's father arrived home unexpectedly. Justin's mom, always mysteriously thrilled to see the man, rushed to prepare an alternative to the cuisine she'd planned, replacing the McDonald's filet-o'-fish and fries with iceberg lettuce and carrots drenched in Green Goddess, and a main course of stringy pasta with venison meatballs, served all fancy, with a bottle of Two Buck Chuck, and a bag of Famous Amos for dessert. She even brought out the shiny white china she'd collected one piece at a time with every twenty-five-dollar purchase at Safeway, using a metal mixing bowl for the sauce, since she hadn't spent enough to collect the serving dishes. Justin seriously doubted she'd ever own the entire set, unless Mickey D's and Jack in the Box participated in the promotion.

Justin's father, Don, was a long-haul trucker, disappearing for weeks on end, crisscrossing the country chasing loads. He specialized in hauling heavy machinery; tractors and backhoes, sometimes even military equipment that tore through transmissions and caved pavement on steamy days. "Tell you what, boy," he'd say to Justin, poking the air with a bottle of Bud to punctuate every word. "There's no stopping my rig. If you're in my way, prepare to be road kill. A pussy-ass Toyota is a Jap speed-bump to my Mack." Don loved all things large. He'd adorned his semi with mud flaps featuring chrome outlines of women sporting colossal breasts. He'd jacked his Dodge Power Wagon with special hydraulics to accommodate monster tires. Even the coffee mug that perched on his dashboard could hold forty-eight ounces. His hairy, once-athletic body, nourished by a steady stream of foamy hops and chemically-enhanced baked goods, had ballooned to wooly mammoth proportions. Long black hair pulled back in an oily ponytail, Don's sense of style favored offensive T-shirts and leather vests; a massive wallet tethered to his belt loop with a chunk of chain. Justin thought his dad looked like an evil biker dude from a 1980s Steven Seagal movie.

He was also a man of unusual opinions, usually hatched late at night on desolate highways while listening to twangy ultra-right-wingers and radio infomercials. Ringo, his favorite Beatle. Hilary Clinton, a serial murderer. The government placed drugs in the meat supply in some kind of mass mind control experiment. Obama and Jay Z had built a secret "colored army" to invade conservative states. He refused to own anything with an Apple logo, it being well-known that Steve Jobs was an alien.

Don also claimed he'd trained to be a Navy Seal, though he'd never been in the military. Told Justin he'd worked as a bounty hunter while still in his teens, though Justin's grandmother clarified he'd spent his summers detailing autos at Hankey Brother's Used Cars. Once, when Don was drinking beer on the deck with his pretend friends, Justin overheard him tell a story about the time he'd had sex with the skinny star of the old TV show *Cheers* in the sleeper compartment in his truck. In Don's world, Shelly Long had a kinky thing for hairy truck drivers and would cruise truck stops on the I-405 looking for hook-ups. He considered himself quite the lady's man, often implying, even around his wife, that the average woman found his overt masculinity overwhelming.

After years of fast backhands and beatings from his father, Justin learned to duck, keep his mouth shut, and stay clear when his dad was in one of those moods. Don's cruelty was as unpredictable as a summer storm, especially when he'd imbibed on more than three beers, or was flying on the amphetamines he gobbled to stay awake while driving.

A few weeks earlier, when Justin had come home carrying a near-perfect report card, dreaming of some kind of "attaboy" from his parents, his father had instead chided him for being a "goddamn nerd," then closed the conversation with a sharp smack to the back of Justin's skull. "Smart only gets you so far," he yelled at his son. "Don't you go thinkin' your shit don't stink just because you got a few stupid A's. You want to be a success in life, you're better off having balls over brains."

Justin's perceived lack of masculinity where his father was concerned was a persistent and painful issue. Over the years, Don would try to toughen-up his son with methods that seemed more torturous than instructive. One Saturday afternoon, wobbly after a few Budweiser's, Don pulled Justin to the backyard to toss a football. When Justin missed a couple of hard passes, his dad became enraged, throwing him to the ground and pummeling him with the ball until he was bloody and crying. Justin's wailing only increased his father's fury, to the point he began kicking him hard in the ribs, only stopping when a neighbor peeked over the fence and yelled, "What in the hell is going on?"

Justin feared the only one in the family more mentally deficient than his father was dear old mom, her face molded in a strange vacant smile when she watched her husband toss him around. Shy and birdlike, she was ill-equipped for parenting, with all her love and affection reserved for her husband, even though Don wasn't the least bit hesitant to slam her against a wall when he felt irritable. When she returned from her cashier's job at Pep Boys, she seemed surprised to see Justin, as if she'd forgotten she had a child.

Most nights she'd dump some form of fast-food dreck onto a plate, sliding it at her son as if feeding an unloved pet. "Did you have a good day, honey?" she'd ask, the question more rhetorical than curious. Not waiting for a response, she'd retreat to the couch for an evening of the Lifetime Network.

The previous week, in a rare move that momentarily smacked of affection, she reached out and pushed back Justin's hair. "What happened, did you get in a fight at school?" she asked, lightly fingering the eggplant colored bruise that spanned his neck and jawline.

Justin was shocked. "Don't you remember?" he wanted to scream. "You were sitting right there on the couch Saturday night when your drunk asshole of a husband slapped me, then dragged me by the neck across the living room, just because I changed the television channel." But Justin just kept silent when it came to discussing his father with her.

He wondered how he'd fared so badly in the parental lottery. He loved reading and math, and breezed through his school work. He listened to Public Radio, devoured newspapers and magazines—and not the ones that featured Jennifer Anniston on the cover, which his mother favored. Yellow-haired and slight in stature, he bore no resemblance to either of his folks. Sometimes, he fantasized he'd been kidnapped as an infant, and his real parents, successful and educated doctors or professors, would return to rescue him. But lately, his senior year just months away, he worried that they wouldn't find him soon enough.

Justin yearned to escape and disappear inside a college library, but Don made it clear that higher education was not in his future. "College is bullshit," he'd announced more than once. "The government just wants to saddle you with a bunch of debt you can't get rid of, so you're beholdin' to them for the rest of your life. Plus, they pump your head full of all kinds of socialist ideas in those places. Better off being your own boss like me." Justin shuddered at the thought of being anything like his father.

One night, Don arrived home unexpectedly, making an announcement at dinner. "Boy, I came home early this week because I have a surprise for you." The hair around Don's mouth was caked with salad dressing, and it occurred to Justin that his father had the dining etiquette of a wood chipper. "Tomorrow we're going hunting.

Head to the Checkerboard with Ted. He's got an elk camp, and we're gonna spend the weekend getting you your first kill."

Don was an avid hunter, spending every autumn weekend tramping through the woods. Justin didn't understand the appeal, and hoped it was something his father would choose not to share. "That's great Dad, but I wouldn't want to slow you guys down. I know how much you like elk hunting. If just you and Ted want to go, I understand."

"For Christ's sake," Don said. "Most boys would do anything to go hunting with their old man. You sit around here with your nose in a book, never doing anything a normal kid does. Time to man-up and get some fresh air. We'll be on the road at six a.m. tomorrow."

The next day, predawn, they loaded mildewed camping equipment and several rifles into his dad's truck. Ted was standing outside his rusty double-wide when they pulled up, drinking steaming liquid out of a dented metal Reddi Electric mug, and wearing a child's stocking cap. Ratty and black with a Hello Kitty logo on the front, it looked like something he'd found in an alley outside a grade school. Ted had long ago abandoned his front lawn as a place for vegetation, and it was now a graveyard for rusting cars and appliances—an ancient washing machine propped sideways at the end of the driveway like a Maytag lawn ornament.

Justin had been surprised his father could attract a friend, until he met Ted, a man that made Don look like a Nobel Laureate. Ted was content to assume the Ed Norton role in their Honeymooner relationship. He threw his gear into the back of the truck and climbed into the passenger seat, pushing Justin to the center. Luckily, Ted was as small as his father was big—Justin always assuming the result of a meth-enriched diet—so it was not too uncomfortable.

Despite the fact that it was 6:30 in the morning, Don and Ted began drinking beer as soon as they hit the interstate, even forcing Justin to take a sip. "When I was your age I'd drink a six pack by myself, then I'd find me some good-lookin' fifteen-year-old nooky,"

Don announced as Ted cackled. "Fact is, I wouldn't mind a little fifteen-year-old nooky this weekend," which made Ted roar as he and Don high-fived.

There was a foot of snow on the ground as they exited the highway at Big Timber and headed into the hills. Ted's uncle owned several hundred acres of timberland, and Ted had come up a week earlier to build a campsite. By the time they started unloading the truck, fresh snow was falling, and Justin could feel the temperature plummet.

"This is going to be a special weekend for you," Don announced, pulling a long rifle from a tattered canvas case. "Take a look. This gun has been in our family for four generations. Originally made to shoot buffalo. Old, probably built in the 1880s. A forty-five-seventy. Worth a ton of dough." He handed it to Justin, different than any gun he'd ever seen. The heavy barrel was octagon-shaped, a foot longer than a normal rifle, with a maple stock worn white on the inside edge. A single shot, it had a wide iron hammer that had to be clicked into position to fire. "It's a family tradition that a boy's first kill is with the buffalo gun," Don continued. "Your granddad and I both did it. Now it's your turn. This weekend you become a man. Kicks like a motherfucker, but that's part of the fun. And I tell you what, anything you hit with this will be dead. If it can take down a buffalo it can take down anything."

Justin had no desire to shoot a gun, much less one that kicks like a motherfucker, but he knew better than to show fear in front of his father. His dad set a beer bottle on a stump fifty yards away, then picked up the rifle. He pulled a circular lever behind the trigger, splitting it at the tail of the barrel, and allowing him to insert a thick shell into the chamber. He had Justin brace one arm on the corner of the truck's tailgate to steady the firearm.

"Put that bottle in the sights, right in the V at the end of the barrel, get that stock lodged into your shoulder tight, take a breath, let it out slowly, and squeeze the trigger. And kablooey—you'll blow the fucker apart."

Justin shuddered in anticipation of the rifle's kick. "Quit shaking like a little girl, and shoot the goddamn bottle," his father said with annoyance. He tried to relax, slowly exhaling as if blowing out a candle, and pulled the trigger.

There was crack that sounded like lightening hitting a tree, and Justin was propelled backward into the snow, as the stock kicked up a couple inches, hitting him in the chin. It felt like he'd been slammed in the shoulder with a sledge hammer, and he could taste blood in his mouth.

"Kablooey." Ted was hopping around, laughing.

Justin was on his back, and Don, laughing too, reached down to take the rifle. "Kablooey is right, but you ain't much of a shot. Missed that bottle by six inches. Still, had it been an elk, you still would have blown him apart. Good job boy."

Justin was on his feet, rubbing his shoulder and face, feeling something warm and unfamiliar. His father had a strange look on his face, and it occurred to him that this was what pride looked like. They walked to the bottle. He'd hit low and to the left, ripping four inches of wood off the stump. His dad put an arm around him. "Don't worry. You'll get to shoot it again. Next time at something moving." That's what Justin was afraid of.

Two hours later, they were jammed into the truck, creeping five miles an hour along a line of cottonwoods that trailed a creek. "Well lookee' there," Don said smiling. Four whitetail deer were grazing near a bend in the stream. Exiting the truck quietly, Don and Ted pulled rifles from the gun rack. Don wrapped the leather sling of his Winchester around his left hand and pulled the gun to his shoulder, dropping down to prop one elbow on the hood of the truck, head settling into his scope. "Get ready for venison steaks," he whispered. Justin stared at the little family, praying his father wouldn't shoot straight. The crack ricocheted off canyon walls, and for a second it appeared he'd missed, as the animals jumped in alarm and bounded into the trees, but the fattest of the group, a female, took three steps and slumped to the ground. Justin had an urge to vomit as Ted cheered and again slapped palms with his dad. "Nice shot, Annie Oakley."

The two men giggled happily as they walked toward the downed deer. The animal's eyes were wide open, still struggling, blood staining out a neck wound. Don nonchalantly chambered another shell, and fired a shot into the deer's skull from his hip. Justin stumbled back as the men continued toward the dead animal. He fought the urge to cry, realizing it would just redirect the savageness to him.

Don unsheathed a wide Buck knife from his belt. He knelt by the deer, rolled it to its back, and plunged the knife high just below the rib cage. There was a whoosh of air escaping, the smell metallic and pungent. "Boy, this being your manhood weekend, you get another treat. It's a family tradition that on your first hunt you get to take a bite out of the heart of the first kill of the day. Something the Indians used to do to their young braves to toughen them up. Transfer all the energy of the animal to you." He carved into the body cavity as blood bubbled and soaked into the snow.

Justin stepped back as his stomach bottomed-out. "You want me to eat the deer's heart?"

Don looked up and smiled. "Not the whole thing. Just take a good-sized bite. It's good for you. Natural. Full of iron. A hell of a lot better than those burgers I know you and your mom eat when I'm out of town." He reached elbow-deep into the deer. There was the sucking sound of water draining from a sink, and he pulled out the heart.

"No." Justin stumbled backward, but Ted grabbed him and pushed him toward the deer.

"C'mon Justin. This is your initiation to manhood." Don grabbed his son with one hand and shoved the bloody heart into his face with the other. "Take a bite. See what it tastes like to be a man."

He continued to smash it against his face, trying to work it into his mouth, finally giving up, pushing Justin back into the snow, while delivering a kick to the seat of his pants that sent him sprawling. When he opened his eyes Don and Ted were standing over him. "You look like a real redskin now," the two convulsing with laughter. "Here, clean yourself up." Don threw him a filthy towel from the back of the truck. While they dressed the deer, Justin scrubbed his face and hands with snow until his skin was sandpapered clean, trying to exorcise the taste of blood and the animal's pleading eyes from his brain.

Driving back to camp, Don and Ted were in high spirits. His father grilled thick venison steaks, served with Wonder Bread, beer, and Jack Daniels. Justin ate silently in a corner of the tent, hoping to be ignored, but with half the Jack downed the two finally turned their attention to him. "So Justin," Ted said, "you're about the age a kid gets his cherry popped. You done the big deed yet?"

Justin thought Ted oozed perviness, constantly finding a way to insert a sexual comment into almost every conversation; the kind of man that society should probably incarcerate just for the disturbing thoughts that rolled around his little head, much less what he would do given the opportunity. "No, I don't have a girlfriend," Justin answered quietly.

"No girlfriend?" Ted's voice rose sarcastically. "That's no excuse. You don't need a girlfriend to get laid. I don't suppose the real reason is you prefer boys? Don," Ted turned his head, "your boy ain't some kind of rump ranger, is he?"

Justin watched his father flash red, and he wasn't sure whether Don's ire would be directed toward Ted or him. "Hell, I don't know what he is," he finally said angrily. "I started fucking when I was twelve, so he don't act like my blood. Sometimes I wonder if some limp-wristed UPS man banged my old lady, and this kid popped out," he said, pointing at his son.

Luckily, the conversation led to a more upbeat discussion of Don's sexual exploits. Justin retreated into his sleeping bag trying to somehow disappear, hoping he would wake up somewhere else. Anywhere else.

The next morning Don and Ted were hung-over, but strangely energetic. Justin assumed there was something about killing that made men more alive. When they opened the tent flap, a heavy mound of snow caved-in. It had continued to come down all night as the temperature fell. "Holy shit, it's a cold one," his father said, as he came back from taking a leak.

Thirty minutes later they were back in the truck, crawling through the snow in low-gear. They inched several miles into a smaller canyon, and Justin began to worry they'd get stuck.

"Boy, you get a special treat today. We're going to drop you at the bottom of this canyon, and Ted and I will drive back up and hike through it. I'm positive there will be elk or a good sized deer in there, and you'll be in the cat bird seat when we drive them out. I'll put you in the perfect position to get your first kill." They stopped at the bottom of the ravine, and Don pulled the buffalo gun out of its case, walking Justin to the base of a big tree.

He motioned at a downed log six feet away. "You can use that to steady yourself." He loaded the rifle and handed it to Justin. "We're going back up, and then we'll walk right down the center of this canyon. Should take an hour or so. Be ready. Those elk will run in front of us, and they have to come right by you." Don motioned at the tail of the canyon. "Don't fuck this up, and don't make any noise. It'll be an easy shot. A short one. And remember what I told you. Get the elk right in the V, take a breath, breathe out easy, squeeze the trigger, and kablooey. Hopefully a big dead bull. And I won't even make you eat the heart on this one." Don raised a gloved finger to his face and mimicked pulling a trigger.

Justin settled in behind the log as they drove away. Initially he was pleased to be alone, but after twenty minutes started shivering. The snow storm was in full gale, and he got up to move around, keeping one eye on the ravine, the valley now a stark white span.

At the one hour mark, he got into position, but didn't see any movement. The temperature continued to fall, and he felt an aching numbness in his hands and feet. After an hour-and-a-half, his toes were stinging icicles about to drop off his feet, and it suddenly occurred to him they might not be coming. Maybe they'd broken down. Or was this some kind of joke, another manhood test? Maybe they're back at camp drinking or sitting in the warm cab of the truck, laughing at the thought of him out here.

Justin thought about what his father said the night before—that he might not be his son. Perhaps he was serious. On more than one occasion, he'd complained about having Justin around. "Boy, you're just lucky your Mom and I are against abortion, cause we sure never planned on having a blood sucker like you around. You can't imagine how expensive it is to have a rug rat, even a pip-squeak," Don would complain. If he really didn't believe they were related, he might be anxious to get rid of him.

He considered his options. Walking back didn't make sense. It was at least ten miles and with this snow he could easily get lost and freeze anyway, and if they were coming back he didn't want to be somewhere they couldn't find him. He could build a fire, but realized he didn't have a match or lighter, and he wasn't sure he could find enough dry wood anyway. He considered finding shelter to weather the storm. Perhaps he could build a snow fort and hunker down. He'd read a story about a mountain climber that saved himself that way, but that guy had a sleeping bag and supplies. For the next twenty minutes, he tramped around the tree trying to stay warm.

At the two-hour mark he heard movement in the trees, the snap of breaking branches, then six massive forms emerged, dark brown and tan rugs against a colorless backdrop. A family of elk, slowly moving through the brush, heads nudging-up to eat low-hanging foliage. Justin pushed down into the log and brought the gun up, scanning for the easiest target. There was a big bull, wide rack on display, bringing up the rear. Justin swung the barrel in the elk's direction, placing him in the V, when he saw more movement to the left. His father and Ted appeared like dark ghosts at the base of the canyon, oblivious to the herd right in front of them. The snowstorm had grown to near white-out conditions, and they probably didn't know they were near Justin's position or approaching the end of the ravine. Justin swung the rifle to ten o'clock, placing his father's form in the V. He suddenly realized what an easy shot it would be, much closer than the elk. Just another hunting accident. An inexperienced boy on his first hunting trip accidentally shoots his father during a blinding storm. Might even be deemed his dad's fault, leaving a boy out here in the snow.

But of course it was a crazy idea, killing your own father. If he was actually his father. The thought of life without Don made him pause. The house would be so peaceful. No more fear. No more bruises for Justin or his mom to camouflage. And next year when he graduated, there wouldn't be anyone to stop him from going to college, from living the life he was supposed to live. From having a real future. But it was nuts. He couldn't possibly...

Justin swung the rifle back to the elk, and the bull seemed to sense the movement, blurting some kind of grunt to alert his family as they moved into deeper brush. For a second Justin considered taking the shot, even if he'd miss, to cover himself with Don. But then he realized he could never shoot something so beautiful, a creature that was just doing all he could to protect himself and his family. And missing the shot would just elicit his dad's wrath.

He rotated the rifle back toward Don, now even closer, placing him in the V, and remembering his instructions. It would be so easy. Take in a breath, let it out slowly, squeeze the trigger, and kablooey.

FAKE GIRLFRIEND

MONICA EVANS WAS NOT thirty-three years old. Nor did she have dense, Cherry Coke-colored, shoulder-length hair. She was far from an athletic size four and showed zero penchant for twice-weekly Pilates in assfabulous Lululemon activewear. Ryan Gosling, not her favorite movie star, and she didn't own a cat named Barney Miller. Lorrie Westfield, not her best friend. Didn't have a sister named Susie, or parents in Fullerton, California. She wasn't a freelance stylist working for Nike. Prosecco, far from her favorite drink. Never listened to Spotify, and didn't own a two-year-old blue and white Mini Cooper convertible, nicknamed Austin Powered. Finally, she was not head over heels crazy for Brian Dailey.

She couldn't be. Because Monica Evans did not exist. She was fictitious, a digital figment of Brian Dailey's imagination. His fake girlfriend.

Brian Daily was real. His online profile a colorless display of facts: thirty-nine years old, a University of Oregon graduate, the controller at Carleton Real Estate. In photos he appeared portly, neck too massive to connect head and body, yellow hair in retreat, always flashing a kind smile. He was usually posed with Daisy, his drooling chocolate lab, in a rural setting suggesting a healthy outdoor lifestyle, which belied his mustard complexion and man-boobs. His wardrobe? Sale-priced short sleeve dress shirts in every shade of blue, topping Dockers purchased a size too large, fulfilling his philosophy of comfort over style.

Brian wrote a blog called Appleflop, ranting against the company he felt had abandoned him. But Apple issues aside, his Facebook posts were infrequent and serene, crafted to avoid negativity. To Brian, digital communications comprised another outlet for his "spread a little love" philosophy: placards promoting human rights and feel-good slogans, flexible puppy photos, and a stream of congratulations to any friend celebrating anything remotely notable. His likes included Carleton Real Estate's website, Bridgeport Brew Pub, two local homeless shelters, and the HBO show *Game of Thrones*. And, of course, his biggest like was reserved for his fake girlfriend, Monica. Since she first appeared in his social networking sphere, she'd dominated Brian's online existence, a storybook romance unfolding for all with internet access.

Apparently, she'd come down with the flu a few days earlier and left the following post: *Hey, wonderful man. Do people know how special you are? That last night you brought me Thai chicken noodle soup and nursed me back to health? Thank you. You are the best boyfriend on the planet!*

Monica's flu had prevented her from attending Carleton Real Estate's Christmas party, just as her unpredictable work schedule made it impossible for her to accompany Brian to any function where friends or coworkers might meet her. They razzed him, but remained nonetheless ecstatic that he'd met someone. Though Brian's romantic world sputtered and splashed, his life overflowed with friends.

To be in Brian's circle was like having a loyal golden retriever twenty feet away, yawning, but ready to serve. The kind of man that multiple people claimed as their "very best friend," the kind-eyed listener, the first call when someone needed to confess, vent, or cry.

As is so often the case, those qualities did not translate into a soul-mate. "It's like dating your minister," remarked the Starbuck's barista that had chanced a night out. "Sweet. He sits across the table and smiles, but there's nothing else. No adventure. No surprise."

Not, however, for lack of romantic effort on Brian's part. He pursued every networking opportunity: friend's fix-ups, singles mixers, group get-togethers, City Club, Blazers Boosters, for some reason a regional hairstylist's convention at The Red Lion. He even crashed wedding receptions, quickly discovering how problematic it is to start a relationship with a lie, as he stumbled to explain his connection to the bride and groom.

Digital romance: Match.com, Tinder, Christian Mingle, even some exploratory work on JDate, despite his Baptist roots. And after years of failure, he concluded love finds you when it's time. But his sister and friends reasoned, as attached people are sometimes apt to do, that loners must be desperately unhappy, always at risk to sink into a sad life of sloppy solitary drunkenness, internet porn, and addictive video games.

"For God's sake, I just don't understand it," his sister Joanne commented during one of their regularly scheduled Saturday afternoon get-togethers at the coffee shop in Powell's Books. "All those bad boys women fall for—lazy, drunken, cheating losers— and here's my brother, nicest guy on the planet, stable job, a few bucks in the bank, all by himself. Lonely. Sad. It isn't fair. Women, they're idiots."

"Please. I'm not lonely or sad. I have a lot of friends. A lot. I'm still young. When it's right, it will happen."

"Sorry little brother, but thirty-nine is a baby step from middle age, when it all starts to unravel. No offense, but the way it's going, it won't be pretty. You need to take better care of yourself. Get some sun. You look like an extra from The Walking Dead. Get that big ass to the gym. There's this thing they do called a sit-up. Try it. Romance doesn't just slide into your life. You need to train for it."

Brian stared at his scone, fuming. He wondered how his surly sister, loose body hidden in her traditional uniform of high waist, acid-washed jeans last deemed stylish at a Duran Duran concert, her hair a rat's nest shoved into a frumpy hat, trained her way to love.

Leaving the book store, he caught a glimpse of himself in the window, his reflection framed next to a life-size cardboard cut-out of Steve Jobs promoting his biography. At the right angle, in the window's reflection it looked like Brian and Mr. Apple were out for a stroll, which brought a smile to Brian's face. Imagine, if he and the founder of the company he detested above all else were actually buddies, roaming the streets of Portland.

Positioning the phone just right, he snapped a picture, did a quick edit, and posted the photo to Instagram and Facebook with this notation. *Big news! The Dark Prince of technology lives! We just had coffee together and plotted the demise of Google.* Within a few minutes there were several "likes" and a couple "WTF's?"

By the time he reached his apartment, a stranger, screen name Johnny Appleseed, posted a comment and sent a friend request. *Maybe not my best photo, but I'd be interested in discussing this Google thing.* ☺ *Steve.*

Brian chalked it up to geek weirdness, but took some pleasure in pondering the idea that Jobs could still be alive. No less plausible than an elderly Elvis living somewhere in Canada, or Walt Disney's head frozen underneath Tomorrowland awaiting the defrost button. Months earlier, Brian read an article by an MIT professor claiming that within a decade humans would be able to download their brains onto hard drives and essentially live forever, albeit housed in microchips and titanium frames. If anyone could have arranged that quantum technology leap, it would have been Jobs. Perhaps his digital ghost was housed in a server farm in Palo Alto, wandering the Web in some kind of iBody, intent on redesigning the galaxy in heavenly white. Brian accepted the friend request, and laughed when he discovered all of Johnny's photos were of half-eaten apples.

At work, the dating pressure peaked on Thursdays. "Hey, Brian, free tomorrow night? C'mon over. Bring a date." His friends and coworkers once again planning some kind of group food exploration: Moroccan barbecue, A Night in Bangkok, Greek fondue. Or cocktail parties inspired by the latest HBO series: Mad Men Martiniville, Soprano Slings, True Bloody Marys, which always led to an in-depth analysis of his social life when he RSVP'd "solo," his female friends flush with concerned, dewy looks.

Of course, he'd love to meet his perfect woman, but he had to admit he found being single satisfying, offering a pleasant sense of orderliness and control. For sure, he didn't harbor those feelings of insecurity that plagued his attached friends.

One day, he read a story about lonely old men scammed by Russian dating services, and realized that an imaginary girlfriend could actually solve many of his problems. Not a long-term solution, but a few months of fake love would offer a welcome respite.

Just to be safe, he used an old laptop so Monica's IP address would not be the same as his. Over the next week, he began to construct his ideal woman, a girl of plusses and buts. Pretty, but not beautiful. Healthy, but not fanatical. Spiritual, but not religious. Worldly, but absent cynicism. Creative, minus the arrogance. Sexy, not slutty. Hip, with traditionalist values. Educated, but never snooty.

Like Brian, she eschewed politics and petty social pressures, embracing the frequent corniness of the web, and expressed deep affection for friends, family, kittens, old John Cusack movies, sleeping-in, inspirational slogans, planet-friendly policies, and when the time was right, Brian.

So as to not make them too suspiciously aligned, she listened to NPR, had a weakness for the "Real Housewives" and "Kardashian" franchises, loved her iPad, and tended to overspend on fashion.

Brian searched obscure Northern European social networking sites to find appropriate pictures of Monica, surmising there was little chance friends would be trolling the web seven thousand miles away. He discovered a Latvian girl (real name Anna), right out of a Neutrogena commercial, fresh fading freckles, button-nosed. He envisioned her waking in muted morning sun, swaddled in white cotton sheets.

Anna worked at The Gap in Riga, and was vain enough to post a stream of photos, often at work as she handled clothing, which Brian positioned as if Monica were on the road working.

It took no time to build a sufficient friend base for her, several hundred random people willing to accept anyone into their inner circle. Soon she had more friends than he did, the benefit of being an attractive woman, Brian surmised. To his amazement, the more Monica posted, the deeper the friendships became.

To add realism, their relationship started slowly. Brian announcing that he'd finally met someone, with a first date story right out of a Tom Hanks flick. "I was walking outside of Nordstrom, and here comes this really cute girl carrying a stack of shoe boxes. She dropped one, they all came tumbling down, I helped her carry them in, and the next thing I know we're at Starbucks in Pioneer Square."

He passed around her Facebook page, encouraging people to friend her with the notation "Brian's pal." Soon Monica was having discussions with Brian's friends, often light-hearted ribbing about their shared affection for him.

"I bet he bought you hand sanitizer for Valentine's Day," his buddy Allen joked, posting a photo of Brian spraying down garbage cans with Trader Joe's lemon disinfectant.

"Gotta love a clean man," Monica replied with a smiley face. "Hand sanitizer and two dozen roses plus a collection of Pablo Neruda poetry. I don't think you know what a rare and romantic friend you have."

She promptly posted a photo of the flowers, which earned him accolades among her female friends; Brian developing a reputation as "quite a catch."

He worked late into the night photo shopping a pictorial history of their relationship, travelling to the beach, romantic spots in the city, locations that would easily allow Monica's insertion next to him, often confusing the strangers he enlisted to take photos framed in odd ways.

After a few weeks, he added an additional dimension, purchasing a second cell phone so Monica could text him. At lunch, or at drinks with Joanna or friends, he'd leave his phone on the table, excuse himself, then text the new phone from the bathroom with short bursts like, Made it to San Fran for the Nike shoot. Missed you the minute you left last night. Can't wait to kiss you. Monica.

"Oooh, Brian, Monica's looking for you," they'd tease when he returned. "She's got it bad."

The cell phone was also useful when Monica was supposed to meet him at dinner or an event. Early in the evening he'd peer at his phone sadly, turn it for the room to see. "Poor Monica, stuck at work, or missed her flight, and she won't be able to make it tonight."

Brian found himself doing something he had seldom done before, lying, as he created the legend of his girlfriend. Monica adored Daisy and all animals, the Belmont food carts, the Laurelhurst Theatre, vintage video games, and spent an entire fifteen minutes examining his childhood collection of Hot Wheels cars without ridicule. Brian grinned as he detailed Monica's intimate side, how he loved the Awapuhi-aroma of her hair, her long tanned legs, and the way she always over-tipped, even when the service was bad.

To be honest, the stories didn't feel false. More like dim childhood memories, like that trip to the beach, the party you think you remember, the movie you saw when you were twelve, all fuzzy and ripe for fill-in, a blurring of fact and fiction. And for the first time, he felt like a functioning adult, no longer that lost and lonely guy.

People began to act as if they knew Monica. "You really need to meet her," a friend announced at a dinner party. "So sweet. Super talented too. You should see the Sketchers commercial she worked on a couple months ago." Brian, baffled, was unable to recall that particular post.

One morning, the receptionist at work waved him down. "I was talking to a friend at Wieden & Kennedy. He knows your girlfriend.

Says that he worked with her on a bunch of Nike projects. She's really good, he told me. Said they were on a shoot with Maria Sharapova and Monica saved the day. Said she's really pretty, too. Course, I knew that from her photos."

A few days later, his sister called. "Hey, I saw your girlfriend today. I was driving up Broadway, and she was standing in front of the Schnitz. I honked and waved. She waved back, but since we haven't officially met it was a bit weird, but I knew her from the photos. I would have pulled over but too much traffic." Brian smiled at the thought of a woman just waiting to cross the street, suddenly assaulted by a scruffy woman in a rusty Tercel, waving and honking like a maniac.

Still, he was struck by the impressive weirdness of it all. The hours people spent digitally interacting with perceived, perhaps fake, friends. The strange compulsion to share secrets online, or embrace relationships that might not exist. Monica's Facebook page had evolved into a collage of other's intimate thoughts: distress over loss, insecurities, often summarized with homespun philosophies. He thought about Johnny Appleseed, who he now communicated with on a daily, sometimes hourly basis. Discussing the merits of open versus closed source software; the future of technology; The Decemberists versus Mumford and Son. Brian often forgot he was talking to a mysterious geek assuming a dead guy's persona. He had no idea if Johnny was male, female, or Job's digitized brain. He could be a smart twelve-year-old, or an incarcerated felon, in this new anonymous world where anyone can be anyone.

His plan had always been to stage a breakup after a month or two; a heartbroken Monica relocating for an unbelievable job opportunity. That would afford him a few more months of peace as the two attempted to make a long-distance relationship work, without the pressure of anyone attempting to meet her, followed by pressure-free months as he grieved the breakup.

But as the weeks passed, Brian became, well, obsessed. A high-tech Henry Higgins, Monica his Eliza. How real could he make her? More than that, he realized for the first time he wasn't lonely. All the advantages of a relationship, without the downsides. They never argued or disagreed. His bathroom remained his own. In some ways, this was better than real.

Monica began sending him gifts at work: plant arrangements, cheese and wine baskets, even a shirt from Nordstrom's. Hey boyfriend, time to graduate to long sleeve shirts with a pattern. Sometimes it was an apology because she was again delayed and would miss an event, but other times just to express her love. Brian occasionally enlisted the help of a waitress from a nearby Burgerville to give voice to his muse. "I'm trying to make this woman at work jealous, so could you call my voice mail and leave a message?"

The next day when Brian arrived at his cubicle, he would casually hit the speaker phone, knowing his big-eared coworkers would eavesdrop in the echo inducing low ceilinged room.

"Brian, it's Monica. I loved that film last night, and dinner was so great. Mmmm, I've got a serious Ken's Pizza jones going now. I'm heading to the airport but called to say I was thinking about you. Let's Facetime tonight."

On Labor Day, Brian took a flight to Orange County, presumably to meet Monica's family for the first time, but checking into the Fullerton Best Western for three days instead. His Facebook posts showed the lovely exterior of an aged but well-maintained white ranchburger, Monica's parents' home, where he was supposedly staying. Outside of Knott's Berry Farm, he had a photo of himself taken next to Monica's smiling parents, actually Mr. and Mrs. Simpson from Boise, Idaho, a social sixty-something-year-old couple he'd met while buying taffy for his coworkers. Mr. Simpson, compact, nicely chiseled with Irish eyes, made for a worthy father. And Mrs. Simpson, well-aged and bubbly, was the kind of mom Monica couldn't wait to visit.

While the Simpsons regaled Brian with details of their upcoming golf outing to Laguna Beach, he envisioned their resume as Monica's parents. Educated, but not Ivy, undergraduates from solid state schools. Monica's dad, a successful CPA, retired, anxious to dote over his two daughters; the kind of man who would appreciate a level-headed son-in-law like Brian with his mutual fund mentality. They'd share a love of numbers and orderliness, absent of the constraints of a too conservative mindset. Mrs. Evans, approachably elegant, a retired high school principal involved in a wide range of charitable work. Brian and Monica would certainly want to spend one week a year vacationing with her parents, perhaps at a condo in Maui over the Christmas holiday.

Brian spent his days wandering Disneyland and other local tourist attractions, photographing the ones he knew Monica would enjoy, usually dining with the Groupons he collected every morning. At night he prepared his posts, carefully inserting Monica before whispering, only half-jokingly, "Good night sweetheart" as he closed his computer. He realized this was the first vacation he had ever taken with a woman.

On day two: *Brian and I are having a wonderful Orange County adventure. The folks are smitten with my new man. Who would have thought it, but we're both big Pluto fans. Just another thing we have in common.* The accompanying photo showed Brian embracing a faux furry cartoon character, the dog's baseball-mitt sized paw planted at the top of his grinning head like a coon skin cap. The post received dozens of likes and sweet variations of "too cute." The only disturbing comment came from Johnny Appleseed. *Be careful of fictional characters. Sometimes they bite.*

Brian returned to a buzz around the office. "So, you met the parents?" Leslie the broker poked him in the arm. "Saw them on Facebook. Cute. Did you do anything else down there? Maybe a little jewelry shopping? A little talk with her Dad? Any news you want to share?" They ribbed him for days, the sweet way in which friends treat people in love.

Brian began to consider the consequences of taking the big step—marriage. As much as he'd always envisioned a traditional wedding, their situation only allowed them to elope. But that might work. He'd always wanted to go to Italy. Maybe even Northern Europe. Perhaps a trip to meet Anna in person, hire her for a day or two for an intensive photo shoot. He'd need wedding pictures. He'd walk into the Gap, act natural, and tell Anna how beautiful she was in the least creepy way possible. Explain he was an aspiring fashion photographer and needed a guide / model to tour the city. He could build up an arsenal of photos, a whole year's worth, the kind he could never create in Photoshop. He and Monica in a church. Monica sitting on his lap. Monica frolicking in a bikini.

In rational moments, he realized it wasn't a long-term solution. At some point the charade would have to end with Monica leaving. Or? He could move to another city, make new friends, and introduce digital Monica as his wife who'd stayed behind for her job while he got settled. And why not? Couples were mobile now, long distance relationships quite common.

That afternoon, a delivery arrived at the office. "Wow, you must have really bowled her over in California," Kim, the receptionist said, and winked as she placed a huge wicker basket on Brian's desk. It was wrapped in cellophane, overflowing with huge gooey cookies, and topped with a flapping red balloon.

Thanks for such a terrific vacation, you Pluto lover. Kisses, Monica.

Brian stared at the card, feeling that familiar rumble below his belt where anxiety lived. He'd been so content lately he'd forgotten that place existed.

He had no idea where this had come from. He fingered the label affixed to the wicker basket. Sweet Town. Sweets for your Sweet. Never heard of it. Never tasted their cookies. Could he have ordered last night, just before he nodded off in front of his computer? Had the one Pale Ale fogged his memory? Sleep shopping? Maybe a Sweet Town flash deal from Amazon Local or Groupon, and in a haze he'd clicked through. He went online to check his credit card transactions. Nothing in the last twenty-four hours. He checked his browser memory, but no record of Sweet Town or any shopping click through.

Still, he must have done it. There was no other explanation. Out of habit he snapped a photo of the basket, then ripped it open and began distributing cookies to his coworkers, taking more shots of them grinning, crumbly stuffed mouths and chocolate-streaked lips, and posted the pictures on his own page.

Beautiful Monica! The entire office sends thanks for your gift. We are all fat and happy!

Brian decided to quit worrying. When he got home, he'd find a mailer with an offer he'd forgotten, and the credit card charge yet to come. Chalk it up to a very early senior moment. An hour later his email chimed. He opened up to a Facebook notification:

Glad you liked the cookies. Save a couple for desert tonight. Grilled salmon! See you around 6:30? Kisses, Monica.

Brian's stomach bottomed. And something else. Something unfamiliar. Fear? Rage?

Someone was fucking with him.

But who? And more than who, how and why? He glanced around, expecting to see a smiling jokester, Brian punked. A victim of good-hearted hilarity. But all heads were buried in work. He rose and strode to the men's room, rubbing the growling fold of fat above his belt. He stood in front of the mirror as the cramp subsided, and washed his hands roughly, as if to scrub away the mystery.

Returning to his desk he pulled up Monica's Facebook page, staring so hard her photo seemed to pixelate, little round pieces of Monica / Anna, vibrating digital tiles fading on the edges. "What are you doing?" he mouthed silently, pulling up the log-in screen, only to discover he was locked out. Flushed, hands shaking, he went to Yahoo mail but found himself locked out again. Someone had changed both the user ID and the password on Monica's accounts.

Stomach rumbling like noisy water pipes, he took quick strides back to the bathroom. He felt paranoid now, inspecting the white bathroom as if he'd never before been there, dropping to his knees to peer under stalls, and throwing open a storage closet. Satisfied he was alone, he caught himself in the mirror again, hairline trimly receding, the second chin he knew so well, and yet, different than just a few minutes ago. His image seemed to float, as if he were being slowly swallowed by a rippling ocean. Gut screaming, he locked himself in a stall just in time to let the tension escape in an awful blast, followed by more scrubbing, hands chapping crimson. Before going out into the main office, he stood silently in the hall, listening, hoping to hear some explanation, then told the receptionist he was sick, and rushed back to his apartment.

Was he somehow doing this to himself? Had he changed the codes in some kind of Bridgeport beer fugue? Given access to someone else? Allowed his security to be breached? Was Monica a prisoner to some Russian hacker, or just his own flawed memory?

He searched his desk for signs of Sweet Town, new codes on slips of paper. Nothing. He pulled up Facebook on Monica's laptop. A few minutes earlier, she'd posted a new entry of herself on a film set, mugging at the camera, her left arm encircling the waist of an equally jubilant man. He was scruffy Hollywood handsome, shadowy two-day beard that looked applied. Casual clothes from expensive designers that screamed "creative guy who makes a lot of money." Brian traced the arm that held Monica close and noticed the trajectory. At that angle the hand would land low behind her. Perhaps on Monica's ass? Is that why she was smiling so widely?

Happy to be working with the great Allen Ducaise, announced the caption.

Allen Ducaise? Probably some fake advertising stage name. Tony from the Bronx pretending to be French, a film school asshole acting the big shot. Of course, Monica wouldn't fall for that kind of…. Brian stopped.

Staring at the photo, he searched for any telltale signs of Photoshop. If this was a mock-up, it was the best he'd ever seen. Arms around waists, intricate hands, far beyond anything he was capable of.

Brian had no idea what to do. He scoured Monica's Facebook page for the next several hours, analyzing each entry, every new friend, each photo, every like and reply, looking any hint as to what was happening. On a hunch at 1:00 a.m. he sent a message to Johnny Appleseed. "Are you doing this?"

Johnny responded within thirty seconds with a simple "?".

Brian finally closed the screen around 3:00 am.

The next morning, there was an email from Monica.

Brian, this is hard, as the last thing in the world I want to do is hurt you. I know I should do it in person, but I just can't bear to see you sad. It would wreck me. But it's just not going to work. As wonderful as it's been, we're not right for each other. We exist in different worlds, desire different things. As incredible as you are, I need a different kind of man, though please understand, I will always love you, even if I am saying goodbye. Kisses for the last time. Monica.

Stunned, Brian sobbed, momentarily stumbling and believing his heart might stop. Then sadness gave way to anger. We exist in different worlds. Yes we do. I live in the real world of flesh and blood, and you… you are my creation. Pure invention. My fake girlfriend. He slammed down the screen of the laptop.

When he reached work, the normally buoyant morning greetings were muffled, a palpable tension infecting the room. His message light kept blinking, an urgent plea from his sister to call her back. He ignored it, sat down, rolling toward his computer. Leslie from accounting approached from behind, wrapping her arms around his neck, and pulling his head to her chest like a mother comforting a five-year-old.

"I'm so sorry. We all are. God, Brian, what happened? Everything seemed to be going so well."

"What? What are you talking about?"

Leslie kneaded his shoulder lightly. "We saw Monica's post a few minutes ago. Oh, God, I can only imagine what you must be going through."

Brian logged onto his computer, clicking to Facebook. Monica had placed another entry, a graphic ☹ over a message sent to all her friends.

Hi all! Just wanted to pass along some sad news. Unfortunately, Brian and I have decided to call it quits. We'll love each other forever, and will always be pals, but sometimes relationships are simply not meant to be. However, one of the greatest things Brian did was to introduce me to so many wonderful people, so I hope we can all still be friends.

There were comments coming in, many from Brian's contacts, expressing support and assuring Monica they were there for her, too.

"Of course," He said, and started to laugh.

"Brian, are you OK?" Leslie's voice rose now with a twinge of fear. Heads popped up from cubicles like confused gophers.

"I'm OK. Actually, very OK," his voice an octave too high.

"As hard as these things are, try not to get bitter. Sometimes…"

Brian interrupted. "Bitter? Bitter against a person you invented? I mean, who gets pissed at Santa Claus or Superman, or mad because you can't date Wonder Woman? Nobody. Because they're not real. This is all some kind of bad joke. It's…"

Carl, the office manager, stepped into the cubicle. "Brian, calm down. You're scaring people. Listen, why don't you take the day off?"

Brian's computer pinged, another message from Facebook. This time Monica stood in front of Nordstrom's, throwing a half wave as she reached for the door.

Best way to get over a breakup? Serious shopping at Nordstrom's annual shoe sale!

As Brian watched, a comment immediately popped up with a "like." *You go, girl! I'd rather have a nice pair of Manolo's than a man any day. Shop till you drop.*

He thought of her, his fake former girlfriend, a few miles away, seated on a purple velvet couch, tan legs extended, red toenails a few inches from the admiring salesman's face as he slid a pair of pumps onto her fictional feet.

Brian sighed, slumped back, and then traipsed slowly to the bathroom. On autopilot, he peered at himself in the mirror, the room looming white and sterile. And in the heart of it, his own face, fading in and out, shimmering, sometimes Brian, sometimes just the space where Brian used to be. Then something clearer came into focus, a happy, confident image, his face thinning, round body transforming, a taller Brian, the kind of man who'd known many women like Monica. He pulled his shoulders back.

Back at his computer, he logged into his own Facebook page. There were comments from friends and several from women he wasn't sure he knew, offering to get together if he "needed to talk." He wondered if the photos he'd posted of Monica would still be there, somewhat surprised to discover everything still in place. As he continued to scroll past the point when Monica was born, there were new photos he had never seen before.

Brian in Cannon Beach with a pretty blonde, the two of them hugging Daisy, and the caption: *Great kite-flying weekend at the coast with my two favorite girls.* Brian centered in an oversized leather booth, wearing a nicely tailored suit he'd never owned, and flanked by a voluptuous brunette he'd never met, two other handsome couples around them, and the caption: *Fabulous weekend in Vegas seeing Elton at Caesar's Palace.*

As he watched, pictures popped onto his timeline, plus a comment appeared from Monica's fictional sister Susie. *Brian, so sorry to hear about you two, but be sure to stay in touch. I'm here if you need me. We will always love you.*

Another from Johnny Appleseed. *Hey, Brian, don't lose heart. Sometimes things just don't work out. Did you ever see the Apple III?* ☺

Brian stared at the icon. He typed, *Johnny, are we real?*

Hah, Brian! Haven't you heard? We all just exist within a dog's dream.

A new picture popped onto his timeline, a bit blurry, obviously a selfie taken with a camera phone. A pretty young Asian woman sat on his couch, one arm around his dog, a bottle of chardonnay dangling from her hand.

Brian, hurry up, Daisy and I have a great dinner ready.

Brian tilted his head back and closed his eyes, then shut down his computer, with absolutely no idea what he might find when he got home.

ONE STAR

SISSY DISCOVERED HER HUSBAND hiding in the back of Dottie's Casino pounding PBR's while feverishly sliding quarters into a Wheel of Fortune poker machine. She scrunched her nose at the musty odor. The building had once been a convenience store, but when it was converted into a tiny gambling hall they'd blacked-out all the windows, eliminating any natural light or circulation. Blaring overhead chillers pumped frosty waves of remanufactured air that stung her nostrils with a slight chemical pang. The only light in the room was the garish red and yellow glow of the clanging poker and Keno contraptions, illuminating a sad crowd that could be a poster for the down-and-out. Mostly retirees, they came for the $1.99 French dip, and stayed to plug their Social Security checks away a quarter at a time.

She could never understand why Danny came to this place, though she supposed he felt at home. He was far from retirement age—only forty-two—but he'd been living off worker's comp for the last year, after tumbling off a ladder while cleaning the windshield on a Kenworth at Jubitz Truck Stop.

She watched him chug his beer, foam-coating the bottom edge of the sparse mustache he'd grown a month earlier. ("Makes me look like a porno star," he'd lasciviously explained to Sissy, though she replied he more resembled a Puerto Rican pimp.) He'd rare back on the handle, yelling "c'mon royal flushy flush," slapping the side of the machine in surprise when he lost. After three busts in a row, Sissy sidled-up next to him.

"This doesn't look like goddamn Home Depot," she said menacingly.

Danny's eyes grew wide and afraid when he saw his wife. He was a wisp of a man, just a smidgen over five-foot-six and 140 pounds, with the shallow chest and skin tone of a meth addict, even though he'd been clean for seven years. Sissy was five-eleven, clocking-in at near double his weight—276 pounds of bad mama jama—and never hesitant to discipline her ferret-faced mate.

"Hey sweetie-pie," he said unconvincingly. "What the hell you doin' here?"

"Well, let's explore that a bit, shall we?" Sissy said mockingly. "Either I had a sudden hankering to throw some money away and dine on shitty chicken wings, or perhaps I was wondering what happened to my husband? You remember him? The man that left at ten a.m. for a quick trip to Home Depot to buy a new mop? Since it's now, what?" Sissy consulted her watch, as there were no clocks in Dottie's, "three p.m.—maybe I was concerned."

She gave him a finger-tap to the side of his head, like she was testing a melon for ripeness. "Could be I'm a sweet wife that's worried about her man." She thumped again. "Or maybe I just know the asshole I married would rather spend his Saturday drinking beer and throwing away our money than having a little quality time with his wife on her birthday." Three more hard flicks to emphasize her point.

"Honey," Danny whined, rubbing his injured skull, "you know I've got a weakness for one-armed bandits. But I'm doin' it for you. I wanted to have plenty of cash tonight for your birthday bash. I was feeling lucky. Thought I might hit something big, and we could stop-off at Ben Bridge for an extra special gift." He made his best attempt at a saintly smile, and Sissy realized her husband had a face that would look at home on one of those CAUTION—A SEX OFFENDER LIVES HERE flyers she sometimes saw in their neighborhood.

She wasn't quite sure why she loved him. Maybe she believed somewhere in his harmless pigeon brain he really was trying to win enough money to buy her a gift. And they both dreamt of a lucky break; some game changer to transport them out of their tough little life into a gentler place. No use being grumpy on your birthday, she reasoned, as she laid a soft hand on his shoulder.

"Glad you was feeling lucky, because you sure as hell ain't getting lucky tonight," she smirked. "Now get your skinny ass home. We're getting dressed-up and going to Pioneer Square for the five-thirty matinee. I want to see the new Adam Sandler. Then I got a Groupon for an Italian joint. Looks elegant, so put on your black Farrah's and that fancy western shirt. And no goddamn hat tonight," she said playfully, pulling off his filthy baseball cap. "If you ain't home and in the shower in ten minutes, I'll find another man that wants a nice date. Maybe he'll get lucky." She bumped his shoulder with a massive buttock.

Danny scrambled for the remaining coins in his tray. "I'm cashing out right now, you big sexy thing. And if there is another guy getting lucky tonight, you just make sure I get to watch," he said with a creepy grin.

God, my husband is such a perv, Sissy thought. *Thank God.*

⁓

THEY WERE IN HIGH spirits as they emerged from the Regal Cinema. Early on, Danny almost ruined the evening, pushing to see Vin Diesel's newest flick, but he gave-in when Sissy reminded him it was her day. The theater served beer and wine, and he redeemed himself by treating her to a large popcorn, Twizzlers, gummy bears, and two glasses of merlot. She loved the movie, which reunited Adam Sandler and Drew Barrymore, her favorite Hollywood couple. Years ago, before she'd morphed into plus size, a couple of her friends told her she resembled Drew.

They walked four blocks into the less gentrified section of Old Town, and discovered Aldo's Italian Bistro wedged between a rough looking gay bar, and a store selling Chinese herbs. Aldo's was only half-full, an ominous sign at 8:00 p.m. on a Saturday night, but Sissy figured it was a new place, so word probably wasn't out. Plus, it was perfect; checkered table cloths, candles sprouting out of wicker-covered wine bottles. She was delighted when they seated them in the small outdoor courtyard, the rough brick wall of the gay bar adding an old-world patina to the experience. A Jack Russell terrier, apparently the official patio dog, sauntered over from his bed in the corner. Sissy reached down to rub behind his ears while mumbling puppy talk. A young waitress approached with menus and apologized for the dog.

"That's Dolly. She's a rescue. I raised her from a puppy. She's really friendly. Goes everywhere with me. Just likes to say hello," she said, pointing a finger at the bed while gently saying, "Back to the corner, Dolly."

"No problem," Sissy replied, "I love 'em so much I went into the dog business.

After the waitress left, she turned to Danny and pulled out her iPhone. "OK, we've got a really good Groupon here. One free entrée with the purchase of another, plus a free tiramisu to split. That's the Italian pudding we love. The entrées have to be of equal value. But I want to splurge tonight and have the veal chop with pasta. Most expensive thing on the menu. You have it too. We'll save almost forty bucks."

"Anything for my birthday girl," Danny said, ordering two glasses of Prosecco to toast his wife, and later splurging on a thirty-dollar bottle of Chianti. Sissy smiled as he preened like a big shot, sloshing the vino around his mouth as if he knew the difference between boxed-wine and Borolo, and pretending that he would actually pay the Visa bill at the end of the month, as Sissy was the real breadwinner in the family.

During dessert he reached across the table and took her hands. "Honey, I've got a big surprise for you. You know how much you always talk about buying a piano, so you could play like you did when you was a little kid?"

Sissy nodded, not sure where this was going.

"Well," Danny said excitedly, "I got you that piano."

She gave him a bewildered look. "You bought a piano?" She grew alarmed as she considered how they'd fit a piano in their tiny one-bedroom place. It was so like Danny to act before thinking. She remembered the previous winter, when someone dumped a broken-down old snowmobile in their parking spot at the apartment. Danny bought it at a garage sale for fifty dollars, never considering they'd need a trailer or some kind of vehicle to haul the thing.

"I'm going to find a good old Ford 150 to fix-up and carry it," he protested, but she insisted he have it hauled away.

He laughed when he noticed the concern in her eyes and whipped a small package out of his pocket. She gasped as she unwrapped a small Pandora charm in the shape of a grand piano and reached across the table to kiss him. She'd been collecting Pandora charms for the last three years, and her bracelet had become her most prized possession. He helped her attach it, placing it between a football helmet (Sissy was a die-hard Seahawks fan), and a tiny bull-dog. She leaned-in to deliver a more intense smooch.

"Darling, I know you've been doing the heavy lifting in our relationship," he said in a low voice. "I know how hard you work. I certainly couldn't groom them doggies all day. One of them would have my arm for lunch," he laughed. "But I intend to do something important, and make it up to you. I've been looking for a location to open my own shop. Be an entrepreneur. Been reading those Donald Trump books, and I think I got it in me. Hopefully it'll happen soon, and I can get us a bigger place and a real piano for your next birthday."

Sissy squeezed her husband's hand. She knew there wasn't a chance in hell he'd ever own his own business. Hell, Jubitz was getting ready to fire him if he hadn't fallen off that ladder, and he was a terrible mechanic. He couldn't keep their old Honda Civic running.

But he made her laugh. Danny reminded her of the scraggly, abused dogs she sometimes groomed on her volunteer day at The Humane Society. Heinz 57's, mixed breeds too ugly to get adopted, but they'd look at her with so much appreciation as she freed them of their filthy, heavy fur, then melt into her when she massaged their rumps, overjoyed to feel a hand that wasn't beating them. Danny was her little Heinz 57.

"I know you will," she purred. "And you know what else? I know a guy that's going to get very lucky when we get home."

Danny beamed, waving for the check, then leaned-in. "That's good news, because I got another gift for you I dared not bring here. But I'll give you a hint. It's big and black and vibrates, and it's waiting in the bed stand. We can both celebrate." She gave him a playful slap.

When their waitress brought the check, Sissy pulled out her phone and opened the Groupon. "We've got a two-for-one here, and free dessert," she said happily.

The girl looked at the phone in distress, and said in an embarrassed tone, "Oh, no, I wish you mentioned that earlier. I'm so sorry, but we only take Groupon on weekdays. If you read at the bottom it says so."

Sissy, in momentary panic, scrolled down the coupon. "Where? I don't see anything about that."

The waitress took the phone, and did a finger-spread to maximize the type. "Here," she said, handing it back. "Read that. It says it's not valid on Friday and Saturday night. I'm so sorry, but that's the rule."

That's the rule. Sissy flushed hot with anger. She was so sick of this shit. Seems there was always a rule to screw over the little guy. Last month she'd walked her credit card payment into the bank first thing in the morning, only to be told it was due at 5:00 p.m. the previous day, so she owed another $57.00.

"That's the rule," the teller said unsympathetically. "Read the fine print on your cardholder agreement."

Who the hell reads the fine print? They want us to make mistakes, so they can charge us, Sissy thought.

"The only reason we came here was because of the Groupon, so I don't understand why you can't honor it," she said angrily.

The girl shook her head sadly. "I'm sorry."

"Listen, it's my wife's birthday, and we choose this place to celebrate because of the Groupon." Danny stood up and loudly joined the conversation.

The tiny waitress cowered as if being beaten, and Sissy realized how young she was, probably only eighteen or nineteen. She had olive skin, Indian or Middle-Eastern, and glanced back at the kitchen with big black eyes as if crying for help.

A tall, slim man sprouting a coarse beard and wearing a chef's jacket approached the table. He put a kind hand on the waitress's shoulder. "It's okay, Ayla." Then he turned to Sissy and Danny.

"Good evening. I'm the owner. Is there a problem I can help with?"

"Damn right there's a problem," Danny barked. Sissy knew her husband was trying to impress her by being the tough guy, which in this case she appreciated. "I brought my wife here for her birthday dinner because of this Groupon, and now she's telling me we can't use it."

Hamid sighed. He knew this coupon thing was a bad idea, but his wife Mina had insisted. "It will bring in a lot of business and generate a lot of cash during these slow times," she'd told him. From what he could tell, it only brought in bargain hunters from Gresham and Salem that ate here once and never returned.

"Sir, I'm sorry, but the coupon clearly states it cannot be used on the weekends. That's our busy time, and to be honest with you, we actually lose money with the Groupon, so we need to make up for it on Friday and Saturday."

"Busy time?" Danny motioned around the place. "If this is busy, you got big problems. What I'm telling you is that we only came here because of it. And I really doubt you lost money. Six bucks each for that shitty champagne. Thirty bucks for wine. That's outrageous, but I ordered it because we thought we got the two-for-one."

"Sir, I'm sorry you feel that way." It was taking all of Hamid's self-control not to tell the pip-squeak to go fuck himself. "But the rule is very clear. However, I do appreciate you coming in for your wife's big day, and as our gift I am happy to credit the dessert. That will at least save you six dollars."

"Six bucks! Big whoop. We were expecting forty dollars off the bill."

"I'm sorry sir, but that's the best I can do." Hamid realized the entire restaurant was watching, and he wanted these people out as soon as possible. But to allow them to use the Groupon was like helping them steal from him.

Danny moved closer to the man, eyeing him suspiciously. "Hey. This is supposedly an Italian restaurant, but you don't look particularly eye-talian to me. And that accent of yours don't sound Italian either."

Hamid's jaw tightened. "I'm of Persian heritage, but a citizen of the UK."

"Persian?" Danny chortled. "Ain't that another word for Arab? Figures. Kind of false advertising, don't you think? Trying to pass Arab food off as Italian."

"I trained as a chef in Rome, before cooking at the finest Italian restaurant in London," Hamid replied in disgust. "I'm sure you've eaten many Italian meals not prepared by native Italians. And Persians are no more Arab than you are. You obviously know nothing about geography or food. And now I would ask that you pay your bill and leave."

"Let me get this straight," Sissy said, rising wobbly after all the wine. "You lie to people, tell them this is an Italian restaurant when you're actually Persian, whatever the hell that is," spitting out the P in Persian. "You lure us in here with a Groupon you refuse to take. And now you're throwing us out of your restaurant. That's fucking unbelievable."

Hamid gripped one of the chairs next to him to contain his anger. "Madame, you failed to read the rules, if in fact you can read. They clearly state you can't use the coupon tonight. I've tried to be accommodating, but you and your husband insult me and utter vulgarities. I'm going to ask you one more time to pay and leave, and if you don't I'm going to call the police."

"The police! Why you goddamn Arab," Danny said, "maybe you and I should..."

"Stop, just stop Danny. It's not worth it," Sissy interjected, shoving a credit card at Hamid. "Let's just pay and get out of this horrible place."

⁓

AFTER LEAVING THE RESTAURANT, they walked four blocks to Kell's Irish Pub to commence some serious drinking. The bar was crowded, but they found a corner table under big screens showing soccer matches and walls dripping with Irish knick-knacks.

"You can't trust a fucking Arab," Danny drunkenly pontificated. "They're all terrorists of some kind. We should export all the assholes that just want to come here and take from real Americans, then lock the place down to keep them out."

"Did you hear that crack, if I can read?" Sissy had switched from wine to tequila, which she knew wasn't a wise choice, but the train had left the station. "How dare that asshole."

"I should've taken him outside," Danny piped in, though they both knew he was ill-suited for any kind of combat.

"I've got a better way to get revenge," Sissy said, pulling out her iPhone and opening the App for DinerRate. "We'll write the worst review ever written about a restaurant and see how he likes it."

Between multiple drinks, Sissy's thumbs whirling, they chalked-up a forty-two-dollar cocktail bill while creating their Aldo's opus. It became the highlight of their evening, both of them laughing and yelling out increasingly insulting barbs.

"Don't forget to put in they serve goat instead of veal," Danny chortled.

When the bartender yelled last call, Sissy pushed "post to DinerRate," then posted it to her Facebook page and several local dining blogs, before they stumbled into the street to take the light rail home.

⤳

THE NEXT DAY, HAMID was waiting at the door when Costco opened, anxious to get an early start. They had twelve reservations for tonight, not bad for a Sunday, and he had to do the work of three employees by the time they opened. He hadn't been able to establish credit with any of the big food distributors, so he made the long trek to Costco twice a week to fill his rolling cart with reams of napkins, toilet paper, condiments, and other essentials. Though it offended his culinary sensibilities—and he'd never admit it to anyone—he often purchased actual food at Costco: hamburger, veal chops, chicken breasts, gigantic tins of tomatoes; sometimes even swordfish steaks when they were on sale and looked reasonably fresh. Even his wine came from here, or the World Market down the street.

He knew no self-respecting chef would dare buy food this way, but had few choices these days. His credit was minimal or non-existent, so he couldn't garner the attention of good vendors. Since he couldn't afford a kitchen staff, he had to do all the buying, prep, and actual cooking himself, which left no time to research and procure the best ingredients, even if he had the money.

He was stuck in an awful cycle of mediocrity. With no budget for marketing, he depended on those horrible half-price coupons to get people in the door, which resulted in a clientele like the Groupon idiots last night; with no appreciation for real cuisine, their dining choices based on cheap and filling. From the woman's girth, it was obvious that she was more inclined to graze than dine. That crowd had little interest in the signature dishes he carefully prepared every night; they wanted pasta and meat. To serve that demographic he needed to keep his costs low so he didn't go broke, which translated to poor quality that wouldn't bring in repeat customers—especially in a foodie town like Portland. He dreaded the reviews he knew were inevitable in The Willamette Week and some of the popular local blogs. One website had already printed "While Aldo's food is only a step-up from The Olive Garden, it's served in a charming setting by a wonderful family." Hardly a ringing endorsement that fills tables.

He never intended for Aldo's employee roster to consist of relatives. With the exception of Luis, who helped clean the kitchen for ten dollars an hour in cash, the restaurant was staffed by Hamid, and his wife and daughter. He felt especially bad for Ayla. A freshman at Portland State, he'd hoped she'd be able to enjoy college life, but instead she put in forty hours or more per week at Aldo's, while trying to maintain a full course load. Despite her hard work, Hamid feared there was no way he would be able to cover tuition next semester. His wife Mina was the bookkeeper / marketing director / hostess / waitress / occasional sous chef; not a job she'd signed-up for either.

It had all seemed so promising two years ago, when a big Seattle restaurateur recruited him from one of the most revered Italian restaurants in London. He'd just assumed the head chef title, and was beginning to garner a lot of attention, when Thomas Burley enticed him to move to Portland.

"Portland's the hottest food scene in America right now," he'd told Hamid. "I have two really successful places in Seattle, and I want to take over Portland. I'll build you a palace, you'll be a partner, and you just keep doing what you do so well." The idea of moving to America, and actually owning a piece of world-class restaurant was too much to resist. Plus, the political situation in London had him worried. Immigrants were flooding into the city, and between the thousands of cameras, and massive security presence, London sometimes felt like a police state. The idea of a low-key life in a clean, liberal city was appealing, and Hamid eagerly uprooted his family, investing his meager savings in the new enterprise.

Thomas did deliver on "the palace," building the obscenely expensive Nero's On the Waterfront, resplendent with a Chihuly glass chandelier and an army of well-dressed valets, but it was exactly the kind of dining experience Portland didn't want. Hamid soon realized that the locals craved farm-to-table tapas washed-down with craft cocktails and Oregon Pinot Noir, served in warmly-lit historic buildings by bearded men sporting inked sleeves. Parking valets were superfluous, as this crowd biked or Ubered to dinner. There was broad disdain for anyplace requiring clothing more formal than Columbia Sportswear or Danner boots.

Perhaps more disappointing was Burley's lack of business acumen. Hamid was shocked to learn his partner's true talent was raising seed capital with oversized promises, not running restaurants. Saddled with debt, Nero's crashed almost immediately. Within six months the doors were shuttered, the Chihuly hauled-off by a burned investor. Hamid was unemployed and nearly broke in a strange new land.

To add insult to injury, the America he'd always considered a bastion of opportunity for immigrants suddenly had a bad case of brown-skin-itis. Anyone born south of Texas was deemed a rapist or murderer, or at the very least a job thief, though Hamid had never met a white applicant for a kitchen job. The most sinister racism was reserved for those of Middle-Eastern and Mediterranean decent. No matter if you were Atheist, Sikh, Jew, Christian, or Buddhist; if you had the wrong skin tone, you were deemed a radical Muslim Jihadist.

Hamid, a lapsed Christian, was born in London after his father emigrated to avoid religious persecution and political upheaval, but now he felt like he'd been thrown back in time to his dad's old conflicts. The only job he could find in Portland was cooking for low wages at a chain restaurant known for its "bottomless bowl of pasta." He liked the city, and desperately wanted to participate in the vibrant food scene and decided to take a risk. He sold their second car, cashed-in his small retirement fund, made the humiliating request to borrow money from his already-strapped father, and tried to open Portland's next great restaurant.

Soon, he discovered his talents were in the kitchen, not running a business. He'd underestimated the difficulty of launching Aldo's, especially in a place so competitive for diners. Four months into the project that left him roaming Costco's aisles, he was terrified for his family's future.

By noon, he was back at Aldo's, backing his dented Toyota 4Runner up to the delivery door. After unpacking the boxes, he discovered Mina and Ayla hunched over the laptop they used for reservations, Mina moaning, "No, no, no."

"What's wrong?"

"What's wrong?" Mina sobbed. "This is what's wrong." She swiveled the computer. The newest DinerRate review for Aldo's filled the screen:

Aldo's Italian Bistro (One out of Five Stars—Me thinks Yech!)

I wish DinerRate allowed negative stars, but since one is the lowest possible rating I'll stick with it. My husband and I went to celebrate my birthday, and it was a disaster from the beginning. Aldo's is in a scary part of town where you might have to dodge rats or muggers. The owners allow filthy stray dogs to roam the place. We had the veal chop—which didn't taste like veal (hope there wasn't a dog missing in the area—though it kind of tasted like goat.). They bill the place as "Italian"—but everyone that works there is Arab—so expect some falafel with your spaghetti. When a huge cockroach ran across the floor, I almost spit out the spoiled lettuce they call a salad (wish I had, as I felt queasy within an hour of eating). At the end of the night they refused to honor our two-for-one coupon, and when we complained, a man that identified himself as the owner (he looked an awful lot like Osama bin Laden—I'm not kidding) threatened us, then threw us out.

This place is a total rip-off, and it feels more like a front for terrorists than a real restaurant.

Hamid couldn't believe what he was reading. "Those are lies," he shouted. "There are no cockroaches. No stray dogs. Those veal chops were excellent quality. We have to get DinerRate to take this down."

"I already tried," Mina said. "I called as soon as I saw it. They said they would look at it, but it was not their policy to edit reviews, and in any case an investigation takes at least two weeks. But we can't wait. I've already had three reservations cancelled for tonight, and no other reservations have come in. And they posted it on other blogs and review sites. Ayla found it on four more sites. It's spreading like a disease. Why didn't you just let them use the Groupon?" she screamed at Hamid.

"Because that would be like letting them steal," Hamid yelled back. "I told you those coupons wouldn't work." But Mina was already out the back door, crying in frustration and anger.

By Tuesday, things had grown more desperate. They were down to a few diners, and more comments had started popping up wherever the review had been posted:

I certainly won't be helping out terrorists by eating in this dump! #boycottAldos

Hopefully the health department will close this place down, and send the Arabs back to the desert. #closeAldos #cameljockiesgohome

⏐

BEFORE THE INCIDENT, MOST of their reviews had been around four stars, with the good service and atmosphere making up for the average food. But people seemed to feed off negativity, and all the reviews downgraded at least a star. Mina decided not to show the comments to Hamid, as she'd never seen him so despondent.

On Thursday night, the restaurant almost empty, Ayla decided she had to take action. She found Sissy's phone number from her reservation, then stepped outside to make the call out of earshot of her parents.

Sissy picked-up on the second ring, and her initial inclination was to hang-up. But the image of Ayla caught between Sissy, Danny, and her father haunted her. Ayla explained the impact of the review and begged them to give the restaurant another try.

"Come Friday night, and everything will be on the house. Even the wine. Order anything you want. All I ask is that you give us a fair shot, and if it's good please post a new review."

Sissy was still upset by Hamid's treatment and comment, but she couldn't help feel pity for the girl. Truth was, while she'd relayed the bad experience to a few friends, she hadn't looked at the review since she put it up, nor in her tequila-fog did she really remember what she'd written. Plus, she seldom experienced a "win" in her life, and somehow it appeared she'd won this battle. Although she wouldn't admit it, she'd enjoyed the place before all the problems. Her food had been delicious.

"Well, I guess if you're serious about a free dinner, we could give you another try. But I hope your father will be more professional this time."

Ayla really had no idea how she would deal with her father. She did know how he'd react if he had to listen to this kind of drivel, but she kept her composure, and set-up an 8:00 p.m. reservation, determined to help her family.

∽

ON FRIDAY NIGHT, DANNY was decked-out in his fancy shirt again, thrilled at the idea of a free meal at Aldo's as they rode the train into the city.

"Guess that Arab bastard underestimated our influence," he pontificated. "He shouldn't have fucked with us. Darlin', we should consider a sideline as restaurant critics. Seems like people really put a lot of stock in our opinion. Might be free meals too."

"Just try to be civil tonight," she said to her husband. "If they're serious about apologizing, we need to give them a shot."

"Hell, I'm damn sweet when everything's on the house. That's what she said, right? Free dinner and wine. Anything we want. I tell you, I saw a fifty-dollar bottle of Chianti on that menu that would go down pretty smooth, and I'm thinking carrot cake and tiramisu for dessert."

It started to rain as they approached Aldo's, and as they rushed for the door Sissy was shocked to see the front window taped in place, large cracks spiraling in a spider web. The wall between the restaurant and the herb store also had a four-foot-wide orange blotch stained into the brick. The building had obviously been tagged, with efforts to remove the paint just coagulating into a fluorescent mess.

Ayla greeted them at the entrance. An hour earlier she'd revealed the plan to her parents, and predictably, her mother thought it was a good idea, and her dad flew into a rage.

"You invited the people that destroyed our business in for a free dinner?" he'd screamed in disbelief.

"If we are to survive, we need to do this," she argued.

Finally, her father retreated into the kitchen, muttering "Do what you want. If you bow down to those idiots, it's on you."

"I know you enjoyed the patio," Ayla said sweetly to Sissy and Danny, "but because of the rain I reserved our best indoor table."

"Long as I get to see that cute little puppy of yours," Sissy replied, leaving Ayla to wonder how her cute little puppy transformed into a filthy stray dog in their review.

"Actually, I was just about to go get her and put her in the office before she gets too wet outside," Ayla answered.

There was only one other couple dining, and the yellow light streaming through the taped window from street lamp cast a dark cross on the floor, giving a sad veneer to the place.

"What happened out front?" Sissy asked.

"Oh," Ayla shook her head, "people are so cruel. Last night someone threw a rock at the window, then they spray painted "terrorist" on the wall. I used paint remover, but it soaked into the brick. I don't know how we'll get it off."

Sissy was shocked. "They're hassling you because of the Arab thing?"

"It's bad," Ayla nodded, eyes welling. "They call-up and say horrible things. They send hateful emails. Dad says they're cowards, and we don't have to worry, but I don't understand. We're from England. It makes no sense." Then forcing a little smile, she said, "Excuse me, I'll get Dolly, and be right back with your menus."

"Danny, we did this," Sissy said after Ayla left.

"What?"

"We destroyed this family. Look," she said, motioning around. "At least before we came here they had a few customers. Now they're under attack. People breaking windows, painting horrible things on their building. It's our fault. We're the ones that called them Arabs. They're not Arab, they're just trying to get by, like us."

"Sweetheart, look at them. They sure as hell ain't English. They might have lived in England, but they look like Mohammad to me. This is their own fault, insulting you like they did."

"No, it's not right." Sissy scrambled for her phone. "I'm going to take that review down right now. They didn't deserve...."

She was interrupted by a scream from the patio. Mina yelled into the kitchen for Hamid, the two of them rushing through the French doors to the deck, with Sissy and Danny trailing. Ayla was collapsed in the corner, sobbing hysterically, Dolly splayed across her lap, as sheets of rain whipped them. The dog was stiff, white foam ringing her mouth. Sissy had seen the same thing years ago while working in a vet's office, when some nut started poisoning dogs in Laurelhurst Park.

"What's wrong with her?" Ayla screamed as she rocked back and forth. "C'mon Dolly. Get up. Get up Dolly. You have to come inside. You're getting all wet. Please Dolly. Get up."

Mina crouched and put her arms around her daughter. Hamid slumped helplessly, then walked to the side of the deck, and picked-up a soggy half-eaten mound of hamburger. There was a large flat rock near the meat, and someone had written "Arabs go back to the desert, or you'll be next" in red marker on the rock, before tossing it with the poison meat over the wall from the alley.

Hamid dropped it in disgust, then fell to his knees behind his wife and daughter, trying to provide shelter from the rain, but knowing his arms would never be wide enough to protect them.

THE TOWER

BARRY HATED CELL PHONES. He shuddered when trapped in a crowd, people yakking at maximum decibel, as if everyone within earshot was buzzed to hear about dysfunctional families, or drunken golf outings. He detested camera phones, users rudely delaying meals to photograph the perfect tuna melt. He considered "selfies" an addiction for the self-obsessed. It saddened him to see couples, heads tilted crotch-ward, abandoning human interaction in favor of text-talk. He'd scream "pay attention" at obtuse blockheads as they attempted to simultaneously type and walk.

But the biggest reason Barry hated them? They'd murdered his wife. Diana was headed downtown in her Toyota Prius when sixteen-year-old Becca Hughes, ignoring the road while texting a friend, ran a stop sign and killed them both.

To add insult to injury, Barry learned of Diana's demise via a cell phone. While he refused to own one, Barry's publicist carried the newest Apple anything, which she handed him after he'd delivered a speech to the Missoula, Montana Rotary Club. "Barry, you need to take this; it's your brother-in-law," she said, her complexion as white as her iPhone 6. Standing in a dark corner of the Holiday Inn, the air a mixture of moldy carpet and baked chicken, a sniffling voice informed him that the only woman he'd ever loved wouldn't be picking him up at the airport in Portland tonight. Not tonight, or any night.

Four days after Diana's funeral, his relatives and friends leaving him to roam an empty house, Barry got uncharacteristically drunk.

He enjoyed a glass of wine now and again, and two or three times a year he might imbibe a cocktail or port. But he prided himself on moderation; maintaining his academic mind for peak performance. With his brain now a snarl of grief and disbelief, he wanted to turn it off. Fog the room. He began with martinis, which translated to shots of vodka since he had no vermouth, followed by his oldest bottle of Cabernet. That's when he remembered the joint, a salacious birthday gift from a friend, stuffed away in the bed stand months earlier. He and Diana had joked about how they'd relive their college years by getting high and listening to Dark Side of the Moon. He toked-up with a long wooden fireplace match, coughed like a lung cancer victim, and stumbled into his backyard.

Barry stared at the new Weber grill, recalling the inaugural barbecue a month earlier, Diana donning her silly chef's apron (Spank the Cook), which had made him laugh. He fell into a lounger, a quarter-full bottle jangling in his right hand, joint in the left, until the wapwap of a bouncing basketball brought him to his feet. Pushing aside the lilacs he watched the neighbor boy shooting hoops in his driveway. He'd known the kid since birth, but paid little attention to children. Shirtless and adolescent-skinny, Barry guessed the boy was fourteen or fifteen, wearing calf-length neon green shorts, a flat-brimmed baseball cap pulled back gangsta-style on his head.

"Hey," Barry mumbled through the bushes.

Startled, the boy said, "Oh, hi Mr. Wells. Sorry, was this bothering you?" He glanced at the ball.

Barry shook his head and took a slug of wine. "What's your name?"

"My name?" The boy squinted in confusion. "Terence. You know me Mr. Wells."

"Terence." Barry nodded. "You grew up fast. How'd you like to make a hundred bucks?"

"A hundred dollars?" Terence looked at him with the proper suspicion due when an adult offers a child money. "Sure, I guess. I mean, what do you want me to do?"

Barry frowned at the empty bottle, flinging it across the lawn. "I have to clean out my house. My wife..." he stopped and shook his head, "she died, and I have to get rid of some of her stuff. I c-can't...I can't look at it." A softball-sized groan rose from the bottom of his lungs, and he dropped head-to-waist to vomit.

Terence gasped. "Jesus, Mr. Wells, you OK? Should I get my mom?"

Barry wiped away spittle, the joint still wedged between two fingers. "No, I'm fine. I feel better."

The boy shoved a bottle of Gatorade through the bushes. "Here."

Barry took a swig, and spat a yellow stream to clear his mouth. "Thanks. All good. Anyway, I could use your help packing up stuff, and like I said, a hundred bucks."

"Mr. Wells, I know about your wife. I was at the funeral with my folks. I'm so sorry. I really liked her. She'd always come out and talk to me whenever I mowed your lawn. I'll help, and you don't need to pay me. You want to do it now?"

Barry blinked hard, Terence appearing holographic as the high-grade Kush kicked in. "Yeah, now's perfect. And I am going to pay you. Always get compensated for your work," he smiled weakly.

For the next hour they packed Diana's clothes into boxes and loaded them into the back of his Audi SUV, Barry sometimes stopping to inspect a piece of clothing, visualizing it on her. He found a stack of fashion magazines, ripping pages to wrap bottles of perfume and keepsakes to be kept. Sometimes he'd pause to inhale her scent before carefully placing them in boxes to be moved to the basement.

"You drive," Barry said, tossing the keys. "We'll go to Goodwill."

"Me? I can't drive a car that nice. And besides, I don't have my license yet."

"Do you know how to drive?"

"Yeah, my Dad taught me, and I'm going to take the test next month. But I'm not legal."

Barry sucked on the joint, and made the sign of the cross in front of Terence. "By the power vested in me by the State of Oregon due to the extreme circumstances we now find ourselves in, I pronounce you a legal driver for the next two hours. There. Drive."

"Wow," Terence said, and shook his head. "Works for me."

Barry stopped to pull a six-pack of Pale Ale out of the refrigerator and popped a top as he slumped in the passenger seat. "Speed it up, I'm not Miss Daisy," he joked sadly as they cruised ten miles an hour under the speed limit. "What's your story? You're what, a sophomore?"

"Junior, this fall."

"Girlfriend?"

"Sort of. Well, not really. There's a girl, and I like her, but she's not my girlfriend."

Barry took a slug of beer. "Teenage romance is the best. Tell her how you feel. Women like that. It goes too fast, so get on it. I met Diana in college, loved her from the minute I saw her, but I was shy. I'd watch her, thinking no way she'd be interested in me, until she finally asked me out. If I could do it again, I'd walk up to her the second I saw her and tell her I loved her. That way I'd have had a little more time with her." Barry belched and shook his head. "Still not sure what she saw in me."

"Aw, Mr. Wells, what do you mean? You're like a famous writer and professor, aren't you? My Dad says you're a big deal."

Barry shook his head. "I teach and write about economics, not the sexiest of subjects. But for some reason that crap is popular now. Diana, she could have had anyone. Somebody a lot more interesting than me. I've spent so much time running around the country, pontificating, when I could have been home with her. Maybe if I'd been..." Barry stared out the window.

At Goodwill, Terence unloaded the boxes while Barry sat in the car, watching his wife's life carted away. When Terence climbed back behind the wheel, Barry was attempting to fire the last bit of roach with the Audi's cigarette lighter, yelping as he seared his index finger. As they drove up Vista Drive, Barry suddenly yelled in anger as they neared Washington Park. "Look. Look at that goddamn thing," pointing at a cell phone tower peeking out the trees. "Drive toward that."

"Mr. Wells, I think we should go home," Terence protested. "I hope you don't mind me saying, but you're pretty fucked up. You should take a nap."

"No, I want to see that thing. The tower that killed my wife." Barry grabbed at the wheel.

Terence grimaced, but veered into the park. At the top of the hill he pulled to the curb, Barry jumping out, half running and half stumbling up the green incline, one hand grasping the remainders from the six-pack. He tripped every few feet, finally reaching the base of the tower. The spider-shaped structure was at least twenty feet in diameter, metal legs buried deep in an oval concrete pad. Barry grabbed a post and shook it violently.

"Aw, Mr. Wells, that won't do anything, and you could hurt yourself," Terence said, reaching for his arm.

Barry continued to assault the post. "I need to blow this fucking thing up. Maybe drive my car into it, before it kills someone else."

"C'mon, Mr. Wells. That won't help, there are hundreds of towers. People will still talk on their cell phones. You can't stop that."

Crimson and sweaty, Barry fell onto the grass. "Jesus. I can't believe this."

Terence popped another beer, handed it to Barry, and sat down next to him. "Yeah, me too, Mr. Wells. I mean, I sure didn't know her like you, but I was around her my whole life. She'd invite me in sometimes after I finished the lawn. Give me cookies or a sandwich.

We'd talk. I could tell her anything. She gave good advice. She loved you, always talked about how smart you were."

Barry took another swig. He tried to remember discussing the boy with Diana, worrying that, as usual, he'd been too self-obsessed to recall the conversation. "I didn't know you two had a relationship."

Terence nodded. "She said you were a big thinker. A genius. That your head was always wrapped around numbers and formulas. Hope you don't mind me saying, but I kinda had a crush on her. Not like you should be jealous. I know she just thought of me as a kid, but… I could see how you'd love her." Terence stared between his knees, voice cracking. "I thought she was the kind of woman I'd want to marry. Smart, pretty, and…"

Barry put an arm around the boy's shoulders, and they sat silent for a moment.

"Did you know she really liked to play basketball? Terence said. "She'd come out to the driveway and we'd play HORSE."

"Diana played basketball? No, I did not know that," Barry smiled in surprise.

"She did, and she was pretty good," Terence said. "She used to beat me, at least until I got bigger. I even made a video of her playing a few weeks ago."

Barry cocked his head. "You have a video of her?"

Terence reached into his pocket and brought out a phone. "Yeah, right here."

Barry froze, staring at the phone. "You could show it to me right now?"

"Sure." Terence opened the video player and handed him the phone. Diana was dressed in gardening shorts and a Blazers cap, ponytail dropping out the back. Barry brought the phone closer. "OK, Terence," she laughed, "prepare to be thoroughly trounced," as she sunk an easy layup. "That's what we call H," Diana doing an animated jig. Barry watched as she worked her way around the driveway. "There's an O and an R," kidding Terence as she made the next two shots, and merrily screaming when she missed the third. "Mulligan," she shouted as Terence protested off-camera. Finally, Diana turned and pointed a finger. "So young man, study this carefully, and someday you might have an A-game too."

Barry gasped as it ended, then hit the play button again. He sat transfixed, the phone in both hands, watching it over and over. His fingers traced the smooth back of the device as he found the switch to bring it to full volume, cradling it as if it were a fragile jewel, a damn cell phone, now the most important object in the world.

HECKLERS

By 7:00 P.M., I was camped out on my favorite stool at Sir Laugh-a-Lot, and still another two hours to spare before my show. But don't mistake this as an act of professionalism; I simply have zero concept of time and suffer no guilt making an audience wait until the room boils with anger and bad karma. Hey, that's just me, with the petulant soul of an artist. Nor am I one of those comics who beg on behalf of the staff. Listen up everyone, make sure you tip these hard working folks who are taking such good care of you. I mean, it's degrading, and really, fuck the staff. I'm not up there to stump for them.

But the day, it'd been easy. A leisurely drive from Seattle, where the previous night I'd killed at a one-nighter at the Improv. I rolled out of bed around 2:00 p.m., checked to see if my bunkmate was breathing. She was, and muttered something about her ass hurting. I snorted a spoonful of my special five-hour energy concoction, and quenched my Mojave-mouth with two cans of Mountain Dew.

In the bathroom mirror, I saw not so much a reflection, as a blurry recollection of myself standing naked in front of the vending machine. We're talking in the wee hours, punching the Mountain Dew button with my erect penis to impress my date. Must've been the only button I could reach, as I'm really a Coke guy, but it didn't matter, I was overjoyed to discover any flavored liquid. After a quick stop at Arby's for some greasy protein, I was on my way to The Rose City.

Sir-Laugh-a-Lot. It's my favorite stop on the Northwest tour. Portland crowds are smart enough to understand my jokes, and stoned enough to laugh. Not like Yakima or Medford where they blank-stare me as if I were reciting the Pythagorean Theorem in ancient Hittite. What I'm saying is that whenever I get more than thirty miles from a college campus, I'm forced to dust off my musty bag of fart and dick jokes to pacify the Natives. Or maybe titillate them with racist or sexist diatribe that would get me ejected from any club in San Francisco.

The real reason to arrive early at Sir-Laugh-a-Lot was the liberal food and drink policy for performers. Most clubs regulate the comic's alcohol intake, lest we reveal the insecure and tortured souls that comprise the wellsprings of our humor. But the guy that owned Sir-Laugh-a-Lot, himself a frustrated comic, allowed free reign. Unfortunately for him, his act was, as Rodney Dangerfield put it, "funny as a heart attack."

Luckily, Mr. B had made a fortune at Nike. Rumor had it he invented yoga pants for women that cured yeast infections, and decided if no club would book him, he'd buy his own. Now he was the permanent Emcee, opening every show with a few painful minutes of keen observational humor. A Seinfeld circa-1984 routine, minus the punch lines. He'd wander onto the faux brick stage in baggy Kirkland jeans and a Tommy Bahama bowling shirt, his bald head festooned with a Blazers cap. Every gag left audiences groaning. The only upside? It was kind of like having Hanson open for The Stones, the crowd even more appreciative of the professionals.

So there I was, lubricating my comedic wheels with shots of Cranberry Stoli. Holly, the bartender and standup-wannabee, seemed mildly fascinated with me. I'd noticed over the last few years that girls under thirty had evolved to the point they no longer had pubic hair, and instead adorned their bodies with blinding colors and piercings. I swear, Holly's spiked hairstyle was dyed the color of the 7-Up logo, her body covered with saucy ink. Young enough to buy me Father's Day gifts, I nonetheless calculated decent odds of cracking open a six-pack of Trojan Magnums with her after the show.

My advantage? Unlike many of the comics that drift through the clubs, I'm a bona fide celebrity, a frequently recognized former sitcom star. My show, *The Maxwell Family*, went off the air when Holly was no doubt still in diapers, but you could still catch it on Hulu. I played Kenny, the oldest son in the Maxwell clan, a loveable but dysfunctional group headed by dad Howard Hessman and an actress best-known for hawking yogurt that makes you crap. America had Cosby-itus in the eighties, and we were a low-rent reaction to all those hollow-hearted, inane, sentimental family shows that dumbed-down the country.

My signature line was, "Hey, I'm just sayin'," which I repeated after every sentence attached to a laugh track.

"Sheila's got a big butt. Hey, I'm just sayin.'"

"Stay out of the bathroom. Dad's been reading. Hey, I'm just sayin.'"

The phrase had become my life's signature line. Complete strangers yelled, "Hey, I'm just sayin'" across bars and airline terminals. Sometimes it was a good thing, like the night at The Comedy Store when a top-heavy redhead whispered, "I've always wanted to fuck you... Hey, I'm just sayin.'" But most of the time it was nails on a chalkboard, a reminder that I hadn't appeared on a television show for decades. Unless you count my seminal performance in a 2009 episode of *Law & Order SVU*, where I played a J. Crew-wearing third grade teacher / pedophile / bon vivant. Pauly Shore ditched the role, concerned that portraying a kiddy-diddler would be bad for his career. Hey, Pauly, news flash; your career has been bad for your career. In any case, I was the only former TV star available in New York within a two-hour window who wasn't repulsed by the character. "An Emmy-worthy performance," according to two drunks and a random tweet that might have come from an actual pedophile. Sadly, it didn't reignite my acting career.

Early on, I was pegged with a reputation for being "difficult," no doubt due to the decade-long cocaine addiction that left me with Keith Richard's septum. I can't remember anything about 1999, other than an ex-expensive wife and a nasty case of genital herpes. My career really nose-dived with the words, Hey, bald Opie, go fuck yourself; advice I offered to Ron Howard on the first day of filming his movie *Parenthood*. Keanu Reeves ended-up butchering the role written for me, but it's all film legend now. And I'm not a guy that holds grudges, except against my agent, Richard Cohen, the swarthy fake-Armani-wearing dwarf. He quit after my outburst, even taking the cowardly tact of doing it by voice mail. The rat bastard called me a "sociopathic no-talent loser who'd shove a Volkswagen into his nose if it would fit." This from a man that had been sucking 10 percent of my lifeblood during my halcyon days. And by the way, if I could garage a vehicle in my nostril it certainly wouldn't be a goddamn Volkswagen.

But word got out, ending my film career. Lucky for me, I'd started as a comic, and really, it's not a bad life. You're your own boss, you can sleep until afternoon, drink and smoke pot during working hours, and discuss masturbating without fear of a lawsuit. Kind of like being a Congressman.

And for all you guys that dream of being famous to get laid, here's a little teaser. Envision how much pussy you think we get, then multiply by three. The kicker is you barely need to be famous. I've got a buddy that works as the weatherman on a station in Butte, Montana and his conquest list would make Wilt Chamberlain proud.

So the notion that Holly might be crooning to see my act in private wasn't a stretch. I threw my best game: hilarious witticisms, name dropping, hints I might be just the guy to progress her career, all while eyeing customers funneling in for better options.

I'd set up a table near the end of the bar to sell my Kenny swag: CDs, Kenny bobble heads, and T-shirts emblazoned with Hey, I'm just sayin'. The early crowd mingled, a few stopping to purchase Kenny-crap keepsakes. An Asian chick, generous in the ass but with a pretty face, smiled, and I filed her as a "possible" if Holly went south. A pudgy couple from Gresham celebrating their fifteenth wedding anniversary insisted I pose for a photo.

At ten-to-nine Mr. B tapped my shoulder. "Hey, Kenny, great to have you back." He shook my hand as if milking a cow. "Great crowd tonight. We've got a bachelorette party booked for the late show," he said with a horny wink. "I want you to meet your opener. The guy is a riot. Unusual. He'll really get them warmed up. Meet Donny Walton."

A tall skinny kid with moppish hair held out a hand. "I'm a huge fan," followed with, "Hey, I'm just sayin'," his cheeks widening into a deranged grin.

I expected better from a comedy professional, and shook my head in disgust. "Yeah, thanks," I muttered. "Have a great set," and turned to Holly with my "what an asshole" face. When I heard Mr. B start the show, I decided to finish my cocktail in the theater so I could get wind of Donny's act. Given his age and appearance, I expected a litany of awkward virgin jokes, heavy on the social networking references. But his routine sprang from a much darker place, as if Hannibal Lecter and Gallagher had mated.

He smashed a chirping cell phone with a sledgehammer after warning people that interruptions would not be tolerated, then ripped apart a Barbie doll while describing in detail the cruel embarrassments he'd suffered at the hands of his ex-girlfriend. He exorcised his Mommy and Daddy issues by dropping a photo of his folks into a Vitamix, pulverizing them while yelling, "Why didn't you use a condom?" He backed over a tiny toy bicycle with a Tonka truck, laughing maniacally as he screamed, "I told you not to ride on the street." A psychotic fucking comedy voodoo witch.

It was shocking and, well, kind of brilliant. The audience, baffled by the carnage, was initially silent, but by the end they were enthralled, laughing and cheering with a standing ovation. I was stunned. I mean, I want my opener to warm-up, not whip the crowd into an Al-Qaeda frenzy.

When Mr. B brought me up, I praised Donny as "an incredible talent," hoping to build camaraderie with the crowd, but it was a disaster from my opening bit. My best jokes, rebuffed. My bluest material hissed at. I tried going local, even stealing a line from Fred Armisen about "Portland, the city where young people go to retire."

Blank stares. Jiggling ice cubes. People rising for the restroom.

Then the heckler started, an enormous bald guy spread across the first row. The kind of man who lifts heavy things for a living, then spends his evenings stammering under the influence of budget beer. "You're not funny. Hey, I'm just saying," he yelled, which got a smattering of applause and more laughs than anything I'd offered up. From that point he was part of the act, nonsensical outbursts that people found hilarious.

Believe me, I've dealt with my share of hecklers; it's a professional liability. Usually they're simple loud-mouths as irritating to the audience as to me. But this crowd, they'd tasted hate, and would've preferred Donny come back and flatten my head with his sledgehammer.

After the show I perched on my stool, Holly attempting to liquefy my sagging spirits. Nobody showed the slightest interest in Kenny-swag, no one wanted an autograph. Even the Asian chick and the couple that "loved me" walked by without a look.

"Wow, rough crowd, huh?" Donny patted my back and slid onto a stool.

I flinched.

"And that guy," Donny said, and pointed at the heckler who had moved into the bar, "what an asshole."

"Not his fault. I died up there. Bad set," I said, downing the fresh shot Holly slid in front of me. "You're tough to follow."

"Hey, I was laughing my ass off. C'mon, you're a legend. Guys like you are the reason guys like me got into this business." Donny suddenly had a semi-angelic look on his face. "Even the greats lose rhythm now and then," he went on. "I opened for Kevin Nealon a couple months ago, and he bombed. No reason for it, just the wrong crowd. You'd have had a great set absent the dickwad. He should've been tossed."

Was he right? Was it possible I'd misread the situation? Sure, Donny's act was unusual, but maybe the heckler had been the problem. I'll admit I'd recently been feeling a little insecure about my material. I knew I needed to freshen things up, but I'd been experiencing a little writer's block since...well, maybe since the Bush administration. Now I was usually the oldest guy in the room, breaking my ass to entertain a club packed with youngsters tapping away at phones buried in their crotches. Sometimes I felt like Bob Hope playing Bonnaroo. A young guy like Donny understood the crowd; knew how to wake up the zombie texters.

But maybe I really was a legend, and didn't need to stress over it. Carlin did his best work late in his career. The thing to do was to put it behind me and gear up for the second show. I doubted a bachelorette party would laugh at someone decapitating Hello Kitty, and without rude interruptions I'd probably kill.

"That redneck, I knew he was trouble the minute I saw him in the parking lot," Donny continued. "I was smoking a spliff when he pulled up. Couldn't miss him. Drives a bright yellow Charger. A loser in midlife crisis."

I twirled on my stool, wobbly as hell, to take another look. Donny grabbed my shoulder to keep me from spinning to my ass. The Heckler was holding court with a group of fellow double-wides. "Asshole," I spat.

"Yep," Donny said. "Maybe we should teach him a lesson."

"Exactly what do you have in mind? Follow his garbage truck around tomorrow to throw off his schedule?"

"I have a way better idea," Donny said. "C'mon."

My initial reaction was to ignore him and dive back into my cocktail. I still had plans to end the evening with Holly, and thought I should do a little damage control after my shitty first set. But then

I considered the situation. For whatever reason Donny seemed to have a little fairy dust floating around his shoulders. Maybe I should put aside my pride and try to learn something new. Perhaps he could teach me about the kind of crowd that applauds seeing ice picks shoved into Kermit the Frog's stuffed esophagus. Donny might be my millennial comedy tutor. And besides, he was growing on me.

We headed through the kitchen to the service entry. Donny grabbed his sledgehammer, and we exited out into the parking lot. He pointed at the lemon-colored Dodge.

"Look at that fucking thing. I guarantee, this guy loves that car more than all other life on this planet." He handed me the sledgehammer. "If it were me I'd bust out his windows, take a dump on the front seat, then set the car on fire. Of course, I can be extreme."

Trust me, the idea of vandalizing someone's car would never have occurred to me if not for Donny. I might suffer many peccadillos, but my illegal acts are limited to sins of the flesh and off-market pharmaceuticals. But no excuses. I was the one that staggered to the Dodge swinging the sledgehammer, caved in the windshield, then crawled on the hood, whipped out the General, and took a whiz through the gaping hole in the glass.

Donny and I stumbled back inside, giggling uncontrollably. For a minute, I flashed back to my early days in the clubs, when I felt like part of a comedy brotherhood; one of the chosen few that possessed the ability to see the humor and absurdity in life that mere mortals missed. I'd drink and joke for hours with the other comics, and sometimes get into major trouble. Maybe I'd closed myself off the last few years. It felt good to have a friend like Donny; a guy that understands the road, and might even help improve my material. Amped up for my show, I downed two cups of black coffee and crawled into the same seat in the back of the theater to watch my new pal's set.

Out the gate, it started identical to the first show, and, as I hoped, this audience had trouble bonding. The bachelorettes, six wholesome girls covered in beads, groaned at most of his jokes. These were women who had loved their Barbies and saw no humor in seeing them torched or raped by PTSD-afflicted GI Joes. Toward the end, though, he changed his act, dropping a screen behind him, and firing up the projector normally used during intermission to show clips of upcoming acts.

"How many of you like crazy You Tube videos?" he yelled. "Well, tonight you get to see one before it goes viral. And this will also prime you for the wild man who's up next. One of my comedy idols. You all know him as one of the stars of that classic show, The Maxwell Family, and you've probably seen his standup on Comedy Central, but I have to tell you… In-person this dude is insane. Knows no bounds. Take a look at what he was up to a half-hour ago."

I was initially confused. Donny had twenty minutes left to his set, and I didn't understand why he would introduce me now. And why the screen? Had he prepared some kind of video homage to me? Favorite clips he'd assembled from The Maxwell Family, maybe intercut with footage from the first set? Was he that big of a fan? He did say I was his idol. But as the video rolled, I immediately recognized the parking lot, lit in a grim yellow haze. I watched myself drunkenly climb on the hood of the Charger, nearly slipping off twice, before caving in the windshield. I didn't remember having so much trouble getting my dick out of my pants, staring at my crotch as if I'd never operated a zipper. I forgot that I'd turned to Donny with a thumbs-up and yelled, Hey, I'm just sayin'. I looked way more pathetic than funny. The confused audience offered uncomfortable laughs and "what the hells."

I probably should have noticed Donny recording the entire spectacle with his phone, but I guess it just didn't occur to me that a fellow comedian would use my impaired condition for cheap laughs and humiliation.

Mr. B roared, "Hey, that's my car," knocking over a drink as he sprang to his feet as he scanned the room for me. I dropped under my table until he'd left, then clam-walked to slip out the side door. But there he was, waiting outside with two steroid-sculpted bouncers. I stammered apologies, attempting to explain that I had no clue it was his car, but that did little to mollify him. It was difficult to explain why I would destroy his ride and urinate on the seats. Between his ranting, and my eventual handcuffed departure in the backseat of a police cruiser, there wasn't a lot to laugh about that night.

Donny was the one that bailed me out the next morning. Too hung over to cold cock him, I shook my head and asked, "Why?"

He looked surprised. "Why? Dude, it's what I do. You of all people should understand. I'm a performance artist. I find humor in places most people never look, and besides, you were fucking brilliant. It seems bad now, but this is incredible. It's all online. Once it hit my site, it was picked up by dozens of others. Jesus, your video has already been watched 380,000 times. Hell, you should be thanking me."

Turns out that Donny ran a fairly large You Tube channel dedicated to just this kind of stuff; *Jackass* meets the prop comic. There were videos of Donny destroying toys, much more involved than what he could get away with on stage. He placed a doll on a tricycle and backed over it with a mini-van. He dropped a lifelike plastic baby out a third story window, pulling what he called an "Eric Clapton." The site was full of videos featuring other idiots like me, setup by Donny to make complete asses out of themselves.

He wasn't entirely wrong. There was some short-term buzz. Two days later, I was flying to LA, booked on Jimmy Kimmel, my first appearance on a nationwide talk show in twenty years. In the bit Jimmy comes out to the parking lot to discover me pissing into his Mercedes' gas tank. But the web's attention span is measured in milliseconds, and after seven million hits my video was replaced by flexible kitties and twerkers, my career in stand-up also over. Every booking, cancelled. Not even the C-level dives would talk to me, all of them citing liability issues. I was damaged goods, and my legal fees, plus the four thousand dollars it cost to fix Mr. B's shitty Charger wiped out my savings.

And so I've moved into a new career in musical theater. Okay, maybe technically it's food service. I'm a waiter at Bernie's Chophouse, but there is a performance aspect. I lead my coworkers in our own hilarious rendition of "Happy Birthday," and if you manage to consume all of "Bernie's Beef Extravaganza," a two-pound mound of meat that will short circuit your nervous system, I'll appear at your table to shower your group with funny stories about your impending heart attack.

The pay is tough, but the stability and regular hours of the new gig are kind of nice. I never have to travel, I'm always home by ten, and usually in bed by midnight—a first for me since I was eight years old. On Thursday nights after work, I pour myself a big scotch, and watch Donny's hit show on HBO—DonnyVision—which is really just a high-budget version of his YouTube channel, except now he gets paid five mill a year. The guy really does have some kind of fairy dust. I read in People Magazine he was just booked to star in a new Coen Brothers movie. Good for him. Like I said, I'm not a guy that holds grudges.

A couple weeks ago the hostess seated a group in my section, and I realized the guy was wearing a Kenny, Hey I'm just sayin' T-shirt. I quickly traded tables with another waiter before they noticed the guy on the shirt looked an awful lot like me.

Nobody ever said the entertainment biz is easy. Hell, Dangerfield was almost sixty before he hit it big. I mean, one of these days some hot director will be watching an old episode of The Maxwell Family and yell, "Get me that guy; he'd be perfect for my new movie." Maybe it will even be that vindictive Bald Opie. Could happen. Hey, I'm just sayin'.

REGARDING YOUR EX-WIFE

AT 3:00 P.M., JERROD and Mark made an executive decision to start the weekend early. Since it was Wednesday, they weren't sure if the day could technically be attached to a weekend, but it was an excuse to break-out the expensive Pappy Van Winkle Mark had received as a Christmas gift. Their motivation to start the ad agency had been to meld their love of partying with a quasi-profession, so the logic seemed sound.

Splashing liberal pours into two coffee cups—one featuring a Starbucks logo and the other emblazoned with World's Shittiest Boss—they adjourned to the tattered couch that filled a corner of Jerrod's office. The space was cluttered with empty beer and wine bottles, and easels propped with storyboards for their new campaign for Maybach Vacuum, a client they'd recently signed. Mark recognized a flattened Styrofoam container from a lunch two weeks earlier, a bulbous insect traversing the brown wilted lettuce leaking out the side.

"So are you?" He waved a crooked finger at Jerrod.

"Am I what?" Jerrod swished the smooth Pappy cheek-to-cheek, as if tasting fine wine. Bourbon nirvana.

"The world's shittiest boss."

Jerrod held up his cup. "Hmm, World's Shittiest is a high mark. I'm obviously pretty bad, because my assistant gave me this for Boss's Day. If I was a good boss she'd have bought me a tie, so I assume I have management issues. I'm drunk or stoned most of the time, and yell a lot. I'm always late. And there's the sexual harassment; I call her

Sugar Tits, and one time she caught me jerking-off to Asian porn. God, that was almost embarrassing. But who can resist a Japanese dominatrix? I am surprised I haven't been sued. But the shittiest boss in the world? I seriously doubt that. Don't you think Putin is probably shittier, or maybe one of those ISIS dudes? Make a mistake and get beheaded. Now I might be the shittiest boss in Oregon, maybe even the Pacific Northwest, but I only aspire to international acclaim.

"Fair point," Mark nodded. "I appreciate your modesty. Do you think we have a brilliant idea on this one?" he motioned at the Maybach ads.

"Well, I'm disappointed you rejected my tagline 'Wow this sucks,' but we're close. Karen's idea of the dog getting vacuumed-up could go viral."

"There's a call for you," Jerrod's assistant interrupted. "Some guy says he's calling regarding your ex-wife."

"Thank you Sugar Tits," Jerrod smiled, reaching for his headset. "Put it through."

"Fuck you, limp dick. Ringing now," she answered brightly.

Jerrod grimaced. "She's incredible," then refilled his cup before answering the phone. "Jerrod Wilkins here," he said in his best fake Michael Caine accent. He listened, then winked at Mark. "Tom, let me see if I understand. You're getting engaged to my ex-wife Sheryl, and you're looking for a reference? Wow, unusual, but smart. Who knows more about a woman than her ex-husband? Happy to help. Kind of a 'man code' thing. What would you like to know?"

Jerrod paced as he listened. "Tom, I assume our conversation will be confidential? Okay, thanks. First, she's a wonderful girl. Congratulations! But I guess we should deal with the troubling stuff. I'm assuming she told you about the addiction issues? No? Nothing about the Percodan, or the shopping thing? She didn't mention that? I'm surprised. Is she still in counseling? Tom, she really needs to see someone at least once a week." He smiled at Tom's response. "Well, the worst was the middle of the night," Jerrod continued. "She'd get that horrible insomnia, followed by the nightmares. Wow. Sometimes I'd wake up and she'd be screaming, and when I'd try to calm her she'd punch me. I don't miss those black eyes. Then she'd wake up, pop a few pills to settle herself down, and start the online shopping. Poor girl didn't remember what she'd bought until the credit card bills came rolling in. Almost bankrupted us. She'd order all kinds of weird stuff: a three-thousand-dollar steam cleaner, horse grooming tools, two hundred Omaha steaks, plane tickets to Iraq. One night she even signed up to be a Scientologist."

Jerrod sat down listening to Tom's response. "Uh huh, I understand your concern, but that's really the worst of it," he continued. "If she could get on top of the sleep, drug, and money issues, she'd make a perfect wife. I'm curious, what did her first two husbands say? What? She didn't mention them? Whew, sounds like you guys need to have a heart-to-heart." Jerrod pantomimed "crazy" as he pointed at the phone. "No, unfortunately I don't have their contact info. Last I heard, her first husband was still in jail. Sure, sorry I couldn't be more help. But I wish you guys the best. Goodbye." Jerrod pulled off his headset and flung it on the desk.

"I've known you fifteen years," Mark said, "and as far as I know, you've never been married. Do you have an ex-wife you forgot to mention?"

"Nope," Jerrod answered. "Could you really envision any woman marrying me?"

"Not really. At least not one that speaks English and wasn't being compensated. So who's Sheryl?"

"No idea. But my guess is she was married to the other Jerrod Wilkins that lives in Portland. Ever meet him? He works at Standard Insurance. Sometimes people get us mixed up."

"And you decided to ruin a potentially beautiful relationship between two strangers as some kind of joke?" Mark said.

"I prefer to think I did him a favor," Jerrod replied. "I'm not a big fan of the marriage thing. Monogamy's unnatural. Someday he'll thank me."

"You know, you might be underestimating your true shittiness," Mark said. "Maybe that cup should say World's Shittiest Human Being."

"Oh partner, you flatter me. That's an exclusive club. Hitler, Oprah, Pol Pot, Cheney, Bill Cosby, the Hamburglar... But I'll certainly keep trying." Jerrod refilled Mark, clinking his World's Shittiest Boss cup in a toast

IMPALA

I WAS ELEVEN YEARS old when the man took us. It was my fault.

Mom made clear we were to be home no later than five, even making us repeat "five o'clock" as if time were a foreign language. But at five-thirty, my little brother Dennis and I were in the arcade in the back of Sunset Bowling Alley, feet glued in place by Ms. Pac-Man's blue and yellow glow. Dennis whined every few minutes, anticipating Mom's fury, but there is no free will between little and big brothers.

Finally, spurred by Ms. Pac-Man's gulping soundtrack and the violent applause of bowling balls cracking pins, I reached level twenty-eight, the highest score in the history of that particular game. I nodded as I entered my signature—GOD—into the name space in the top slot, and called it quits.

As we were leaving, I noticed the man standing at the counter, handing in his bowling shoes. It was the long stringy hair and tattered army field jacket that first grabbed my attention, the street uniform of the Vietnam vets that had been roaming around the last few years. When he turned, I blanched at his skeletal face, eyes half-lidded, and envisioned Bruce Dern, the man who killed John Wayne in *The Cowboys*. I didn't notice him follow us out, so I didn't know it was him who grabbed us as we unlocked our Huffys' from the light pole, his boney fingers digging into the napes of our necks and rushing us like cattle through a chute into that deep car trunk.

Dennis cried out, and the man slapped him hard on a fat moist cheek, stunning us into submission.

"Shut the fuck up or I'll cut your goddamn head off," he said in a low serious voice. I wrapped my arm around my brother's face, urging him to be quiet when the lid slammed us into darkness. As the car moved onto the street, we bounced hard on spongy shocks, damp rusty grit covering my cheek, air thick with oil and some other rotting smell. Sometimes I heard a muffled hum from the radio, Credence Clearwater Revival, the man singing along out-of-tune to "Fortunate Son."

After maybe twenty minutes, we stopped, the brakes grating. I heard him get out of the car, a garage door rolling up, then rolling back down after we'd moved in. When the trunk opened bright light streamed in, the terror subsiding momentarily. It was a garage like any other, a place where normal men like our dad stowed their stuff: a lawn mower in the corner, rakes and tools hanging neatly on pegs, a boxy freezer humming against the wall. But Dennis flew into a panic, springing out as if he might take flight, a caged bird suddenly freed. The man grabbed him, yelled, "Shut the fuck up. I warned you," and slammed him down outside of my sight line. I collapsed at the front of the car, covering my eyes when the man grabbed the short, square-headed shovel off the wall, swinging it as if he were about to bust-up stubborn dirt clods.

Impala. I concentrated on the chrome emblem on the car's grill, trying to block out the sheaving sound, metal into thick mud, and the more horrible silence when my brother stopped screaming. The man rushed to the front of the car and grabbed me by the hair, bloody shovel dangling in his left hand, and dragged me into the basement.

And that was the last time I was above ground for nine years.

Thirty-three hundred days. Eighty thousand hours. Five million minutes. I had plenty of time to do the math, to learn every inch of that twelve-by-twelve room. Fresh hospital-green paint and gray linoleum, a new porcelain sink and toilet in the corner. I knew I wasn't the first. I crawled on the floor like a slug, forensically analyzing every inch of the walls, spent hours splayed on my back under the bed pretending the crisscross of the box springs were clouds. I imagined our family in Pioneer Park, our parents laughing as Dennis and I struggled to get a kite airborne.

It was there I discovered the person imprisoned before me. He— was it a he?—I always assumed so, had notched two hundred and forty-one scratches, four vertical with the fifth a cross scratch, on the metal slats. Did he escape? Or was his time up? I counted days in my head until I could no longer keep track, panicking when I thought I might be close to that number.

Sometimes the man brought me comic books, and I'd pretend they were letters from home; Archie and Jughead updating me on what was happening with the gang in Riverdale. After maybe a year, he started rolling in a black-and-white television for an hour or two every few days, just never at a time when I could see news or anything about the outside world. Reception was almost non-existent, but I'd twist and turn the rabbit ears to watch snowy episodes of Gilligan's Island, wishing I was trapped on an island instead of here, swinging in a hammock and eating coconuts with the Skipper.

Sometimes the man would even watch with me. He'd hear me giggle and slip in quietly to stand in the corner, a strange smile on his face as if he were witnessing something magical. He might have cookies or chocolates wrapped in a napkin, and he'd cautiously hand me one, gesturing toward his lips as if I didn't know how to eat, then grin happily when I chewed and smiled at the sweetness.

After a while, I couldn't comprehend time, didn't know how old I was or how long I'd been locked away. At some point the man gave me an electric razor and told me to shave every other day, though he wouldn't allow a mirror. My hands traced my face, the strange new sensation of whiskers, chubby cheeks now slim, trying to comprehend what I might look like.

I'd speak to make sure I still could, to hear the changes in my voice as it grew deeper. Eventually, I forgot my parents and friends, my thoughts confined to Dennis and the one who'd made the notches.

Praying I'd misunderstood what had transpired in the garage, I'd talk to my brother for hours on the off-chance that he might be in the next room with his ear to the wall.

With a lot of time to think, you think a lot about time, and I often considered the importance of minutes. If only I'd followed my mother's instructions and left a few minutes earlier, we wouldn't be here. If it had taken me a few minutes longer to beat Ms. Pac-Man, the man wouldn't have seen us. Sometimes I'd lie under the bed and carry-on long discussions with the one who came before me, the only one who could really understand it all.

That's where I was when an explosion upstairs rattled the foundation. It sounded like a bulldozer had brought down a wall. I jumped up and moved to the back of the room as the hallway filled with angry shouting. My door burst apart at the frame, a helmeted man in black, with what looked like a cannon swinging from his arms, yelling at me to get on the ground. Then other uniformed men brandishing huge weapons rushed in. I couldn't comprehend what was happening and thought they might be aliens. Like War of the Worlds, perhaps the earth had been overrun by creatures from another planet and the man and I were the last holdouts. Had he actually been trying to save me?

They whisked me from the basement into a sinister-looking van, and for the next twenty-four hours I rotated between hospitals and a police station. I soon understood the truth. I was now a twenty-year-old man that had spent almost half his life in a cellar imagining he was friends with Veronica and Richie Rich, and communing with dead people.

My mother was gone. Some suspected suicide, with Mom so grief stricken that late one night six years earlier she drove head-on into a telephone pole. My father had remarried, filled his house with new children, and after my initial homecoming he didn't seem overly interested in seeing me, an unexpected, painful relic from a time he'd rather forget.

I was famous for a few weeks, even appearing on the cover of People Magazine, "The Boy in the Basement." But horrifying stories like mine have a short shelf life, and I was soon replaced in the public's imagination by a British movie star caught communing with a male prostitute, and a Nebraska woman that gave birth two dozen times.

Society loves blame, and officials that should have found me right after the abduction lost their jobs. Friends and classmates I barely remembered, now in college or living their lives, threw a party and paraded me around like a science exhibit.

Of course, there was counseling and concern, but I felt more like a specimen, voyeuristic doctors repeatedly urging me to confront the worst details. Those that made their livings documenting monstrous crimes hovered around with the promise of fame and money, neither of which I craved. I had no desire to be the star of a freak show. I understood that everyone assumed a boy held in solitary confinement for half his life had to be insane, and people feared me almost as much as they did the man. I'd been branded.

I suppose I could have gone back to school or learned some kind of trade, but mostly I just wanted to keep moving. For a while I tried to relate, to be human, but the world didn't seem any more real than those comic books, and I found myself drawn to ugly places that reminded me of the room. Counselors and psychologists expressed a grim understanding of my choices, my hollowness. I was defined by my diagnosis: post-traumatic stress and sociopathic tendencies brought on by years of captivity. And I suppose that at some point even a compassionate society has to enforce its own rules and laws.

In Solvang, California, I was arrested for assault and armed robbery. My victim only spent one night in the hospital, but it cost me a year in prison. Next they sent me to a halfway house and a job I refused to work, the hairnet and paper hat the last straw. I left for Texas, where they were less forgiving after I shoved a beer bottle into a man's ear, landing me in an even smaller room for three years. In Colorado, four years for drugs and a stolen Glock. In Idaho, I made a decent living robbing truck stops and convenience stores, racking up another half decade in an institution surrounded by fir trees. After that I worked my way back home to Montana, even though there was nobody there I wanted to see. That's where I went big time, seventy-five to life for killing a bartender in Great Falls. Did I feel remorse for the man I murdered, the people I hurt? They were no more real to me than those blue and yellow circles I used to gobble-up with Ms. Pac Man. I wasn't even sure I existed. I sometime considered it a distinct possibility that this was all a mirage, and I was still in the basement.

Montana has only one prison, Deer Lodge, a red-stoned fortress straight out of a medieval nightmare, built in 1871 as the territorial lock-up. You might've thought someone would do a little research, realize who I was, and decide it might not be a great idea to incarcerate me in the same joint as the man who kept me captive for all that time. Maybe they'd forgotten. It had been over twenty years, and he was growing old serving three consecutive life sentences, locked-up in solitary when I arrived, so perhaps they thought it wouldn't be an issue. Might have even seen me as a solution, an easy way to trim the herd, assuming I would certainly kill him and save the taxpayers some money.

In my fifth year at Deer Lodge, they released the man back into general population. I spotted him across the yard, head down, smoking cigarettes and shuffling back and forth on a six-foot stretch near the wall. He was smaller than I remembered, and had to be pushing sixty, skinny and feeble, thin-stretched skin the color of cigarette ash. I doubted he recognized me after all this time.

I became the scientist, and he my lab rat. He was always alone, eyes locked on his feet, only raising his gaze to keep from walking into a wall. I memorized his patterns, watched him retreat to the same safe space every day, carrying his tray to the back of the cafeteria to eat alone. I never saw him speak, an occasional nod the only acknowledgement of an outside world.

For a while I imagined what I could do to him, the various ways I might end his life. Sometimes the fantasy was brutal, dousing him in lighter fluid and sparking him up like a torch, or something slower, my knee hard on his sternum, his eyes bulging in recognition as I slowly strangled him. Or a shiv pounded into his center as he watched the life leak out. But gradually, playing out every violent scenario, the urge to kill subsided, and I remained content just to watch, curious about what made him tick.

When I was in the basement, I'd spend my time anticipating his sound, my internal clock resetting to the man's rhythms, the weight of his steps foretelling how the visit might unfold. If he walked angrily, gait heavy and hard, sometimes cursing while he unlocked the door, I knew the day had gone bad and I would pay the price. I'd retreat to the corner, pushing in hard and covering my head, wondering if this might be the time he went too far. Other nights he'd sneak in lightly with a soft murmur, intent on using me to fill some other void, offering what he probably assumed was tenderness. Some nights he could be almost childlike, a gentle big brother come to play.

I heard from one of the cafeteria workers that he had stage-four lung cancer, a believable diagnosis given the hollow coughs and thick phlegm he was always hacking up. His movements lapsed to half-speed, his complexion the pale hue of the dying. I knew he would soon be moved to hospice to be pumped full of morphine for his final days, a death that seemed unfairly peaceful for a felon of his accomplishments. So I decided to sit down across from him in the cafeteria as he took slow spoonfuls of soup.

He looked up without surprise, anticipating me.

"Do you know who I am?" I asked. He nodded slowly, then stared down at his bowl and continued to eat. Up close, his shoulders were narrow, a brittle, deflated version of the terrifying specter that had shoved us into that trunk. We sat in silence; the only sound him slurping his soup. Finally, he put down the spoon and looked at me with a slight grin, as if we were old friends.

"You and me boy, we just never really left that house, did we?"

And I realized he was right. In some crazy way, I would always be there, my head pushing into the car's grill, Impala burned into my brain, or lying under that bed, looking into the clouds of my imagination, wondering when I would hear him unlock the door.

JESUS KNOCKING

CALEB ALWAYS SITS ON the aisle, third row, at the 9:00 a.m. Sunday service, close enough to marvel as Pastor Dan fills with Jesus, but far enough back he won't be hit by any Holy Ghost shrapnel. He never misses a Sunday. It's a wondrous thing to see God inhabit a man's body.

"Welcome all you magnificent sinners," Pastor Dan booms in Barry White baritone, smiling wide as the crowd shuffles in. He greets every parishioner by name, grasping hands, left palm sliding to cup an elbow. It's the Pastor Dan signature hug, face close, delivered with candy cane breath. Mrs. Dan and their two youngsters stand five feet back, echoing every pleasantry.

Ugly by traditional standards, the pores on Pastor Dan's nose are wide enough to garage a Buick, his bald head a cranial topographic map, shocking at first, but over time it makes him appear otherworldly. He's a school bus of a man, crevassed black marble skin covered with three piece suits that highlight his corpulence; yellow, arctic white, circus colors not usually seen in men's clothing, but Pastor Dan has no fear.

"I'm a billboard for Jesus," he hollers. "The Lord wants you to see me, so I can introduce the two of you. C'mon now," he laughs wildly. "Meet the Lord. Say hi to Daddy."

Sweat pools at the base of his inner tube neck. Caleb rises an inch in his seat, knowing God Almighty is about to make his entrance. Pastor Dan breaks into a James Brown boogie, and takes a swig of Jesus juice—actually Two Buck Chuck Merlot in a brass chalice.

"Blood of Christ. BLOOD of Christ. Fill me Jesus. I am your vessel." He hollers and gyrates, and the congregation breathes hard, assuming a heart attack imminent; no man his size should move that way. Dan snaps back and freezes, staring into some unseen plane. Caleb swears up and down Dan's brown eyes turn blue as the Lord takes hold. And for the next hour, he's big black Jesus. God's only son in neon polyester with marble-sized diamond rings and a gold crucifix big enough to top a steeple. Notorious Biggy Hey-Zuse.

And man, can this Jesus hold a room! Mesmerizing. He starts with a few of his greatest hits: love your neighbor, help the poor, honor his dad. A parable or two, Caleb a big fan of the prodigal son. Then it's down to business.

"I want you to go spread my word. Stop your neighbors on the street. Tell them about me. Bang on doors. Don't be afraid. Tell them it's Jesus knocking. That the only path to heaven is to know me, and they need to embrace me as their savior. It's the only way they'll know the glory of heaven. And oh, oh, …you're gonna' like heaven."

He smiles as if he's about to reveal life's greatest mystery, voice dropping to a whisper, "Brothers and sisters, what a time we're going to have. Heaven's better than you ever imagined. Jars full of the most delicious chocolate chip cookies you've ever tasted. Free. Eat all you want cause nobody gets fat," he sloshes his liquid belly and giggles. "You won't recognize me there. Evvverybody's beautiful up there. In heaven, I look just like Denzel. And you, Mrs. Lackman," he points at the spindly woman in the front row, "look exactly like Miss Audrey Hepburn."

A little laugh and then a cheer emanates from the crowd. "No sickness in heaven," he points at Mrs. Scott's walker. "No need for those kind of appliances. Everyone walks, heck, everyone runs if they so choose in heaven." The crowd smiles. "No pain where we're going. Not for your body or your mind. Wake up every day feeling like you're twelve years old and headed to the carnival! And money? Don't need it. Eveeerybody's rich in heaven."

And to Caleb's amazement, this room full of poor white people begins to cheer and applaud. Gnarled loggers, reformed meth heads, mountain hermits, gun-toting bigots, ancient widows preparing for the abyss, camo-covered rednecks, families whose home address is a walled tent...all gathered in a peeling double wide, asses on plank benches, screaming praise to a fat black man in a yellow suit channeling Jesus. Who'd have thunk it?

Certainly not Caleb. Nor would he have ever thought he would be among them, clapping and yelling like a fool.

⌒

EIGHTEEN MONTHS EARLIER, CALEB was buying jerky and a six pack at The Mart when he first met Pastor Dan. Rare to see a black man in Carson, Washington—much less a Kenworth-sized one—styling a lime green jump suit, a cantaloupe lodged under one arm. Caleb eyed him curiously, wondering if he might be one of the judges on that show with Christina Aguilera and the singers. He didn't really know the program but thought Christina was fine. Only someone famous would dare dress that way. Plus, this wasn't the place to buy any kind of fruit or vegetable. Stick to stuff in cans or sealed bags with long expiration dates.

"How are you, my young friend?" The man approached and extended a meaty paw, gold bracelets jangling like wind chimes. Caleb couldn't remember ever touching a black person. He'd tried once at a dance club in Portland—Budweiser-encouraged—almost brushing his forearm across the perfect backside of a Beyoncé look-alike on the dance floor, but stopped when he nearly got his head bashed-in by her linebacker boyfriend.

He stared at the pinkish palm, curious if it would be rough and dry like snakeskin. When he took it, the man pulled him close, and for a second Caleb feared he was going to hug him, or worse, consume him like an alien body snatcher. But the hand was warm and soft, and as the other hand moved to Caleb's elbow, he felt comforted, like a baby tucked tight on his mama's bosom. He couldn't explain it, but from that day forward, whenever he was around Pastor Dan, he was soothed.

"Very happy to meet you. This looks like a perfect day for a cold beer." He motioned at Caleb's six pack. "Can I assume you're a native of this fine town?"

Caleb had never heard Carson referred to as fine. Wasn't sure it even qualified as a town, as the sign said "Carson—Unincorporated" which meant it was really just a four-block-long outpost of grayed buildings, half abandoned, that nobody claimed. There was still a hardware store, a bar, a tired cafe, and The Mart, but most of the structures had been empty for decades.

Caleb was third generation in Carson, at twenty-two too young to remember his grandfather's good days, when Skamania County was flush with cash from timber contracts, and Carson was a rich little burg with a good school and a happy middle class. He hadn't been born yet when it ended, sometime in the early eighties, when recession, foreign competition, and "the goddamn little bird," as his Dad referred to the spotted owl, dried up the logging community. However, he was here to live the decline, his father and most of the other men in the area still in their working prime, now bitter and unemployed, with few prospects for men wielding chainsaws.

Hating, drinking, and sometimes stealing became the main professions for that generation. The three not being a good mix, people weren't surprised six years ago when Caleb's dad had been shot dead during a drunken burglary. Nobody really thought Caleb's father was the criminal-type, but under the influence he seemed to lose all common sense, and after a long night sucking-down beers at The Bungalow, he chose the wrong barn to rob, the old farmer that owned the place greeting the trespasser with a twelve-gauge.

In honest moments, Caleb and his family would admit they didn't much miss him. During his last few years, his father lived like a man with a terminal disease eating him from inside. He'd lash out, with words, sometimes fists, sloppy and unpredictable. Some nights, his Mom would get a call at 2:00 a.m. from The Bungalow, the bartender asking her to retrieve the man sleeping at the end of the bar. Caleb had no memory of the person she'd once loved, the handsome Stevenson High sweetheart she'd started dating at fourteen. The house became calm when he was gone, his $50,000 life insurance policy smoothing over any residual grief.

Caleb, nowhere to go, stayed around to take care of his mom and sister. His mother, no longer the petite, pretty woman with an easy smile, had ballooned to near twice her original size, spending her days gorging on cheap fluorescent baked goods, watching reality shows as if visiting family, and working part-time at the Rural Cooperative. His sister Lynn, five years his junior and finishing high school, consumed a similar diet, and had just been diagnosed with early onset juvenile diabetes, a disease that worked the community like the flu.

Caleb sometimes worried that his father's criminal inclinations and alcoholism might be hereditary. He had higher ambitions, so he tried to infuse discipline in his life. Went easy on the beer. Ordered salad instead of fries. Ran two miles every morning. Owned a Kindle that contained Dale Carnegie and Donald Trump's how-to manuals, plus *The Seven Habits of Highly Effective People*, since he planned to be highly effective in his life. He had a Visa card from his credit union, which he paid in full every month. When his Dad died, he hauled off the old appliances and the rusting Dodge that had barricaded the lawn for as long as they could remember, and now kept the house tidy and painted his mom's favorite robin's egg blue.

Against the odds Caleb emerged an optimist, the likeable and dependable sort, not afraid to say hello to anyone, with a reasonable gift of gab. His mother would sometimes say to him, "Caleb, not quite sure why the sun always shines in your world, but good for you."

Though he didn't graduate at the top of his class, he had reasonable grades, and worked the night shift at Joe's El Rio Café while taking classes at the local community college, earning an Associate's Degree in Computer Networking. With a stroke of luck, he got on as a lineman for Century Link, installing phone and internet service. At twenty-five bucks an hour with a retirement plan, he was a high flyer in Carson, plenty of cash to go into Hood River or Portland on the weekends, make the payments on a sweet Toyota Tacoma that he used to haul his wind surfing equipment, and buy his Mom a new refrigerator at Best Buy.

So yes, he was as native as you could be in Carson.

Pastor Dan introduced himself and explained he was getting ready to reopen the old Baptist Church on the edge of town. Caleb drove by the worn structure every day, and couldn't recall it ever being occupied. He'd always assumed one day it would just burn to the ground, as buildings were apt to do in Carson. Surprising enough anyone would take it over, let alone a big black dude. In this town folks tended to be suspicious, with the only acceptable black being the color of their gun rack.

"Come one, come all. Baptist, Catholic, Jew. Even atheist!" Big Pastor Dan smile. "All are welcome to sit with their neighbors, enjoy a little fellowship. Can I ask you, young man, what's your relationship with Jesus?"

Ah, here we go. Recruiting. Several of Caleb's schoolmates were Jehovah's Witnesses, and they'd put the rush on him, especially after his dad died. A couple years earlier while walking in downtown Portland, a pretty Scientologist girl that looked a lot like Scarlett Johansson tried to get him to go into one of their Celebrity Centers. If a cute blonde with a cherry ass couldn't convert him, this guy didn't have a chance.

But just to be neighborly he said, "Can't say I have a relationship. My mom's a believer. Goes to church in Stevenson sometimes, but I'm not one much for organized religion."

"Me either." Another Pastor Dan chuckle. "My church is pretty disorganized. We get together as a community, listen to a little music.

You like music? We even dance a bit. The Lord gave us legs to dance. It's just nice to fill your soul on a Sunday morning."

Lulled by the deep bass voice, Caleb watched the big man's lips move. This is probably how God sounds. Twenty minutes later, the two were in the parking lot by Caleb's truck, drinking beer, passers-by gawking at the strange twosome.

"God wouldn't have made something so delicious if he didn't intend for us drink it," Pastor Dan smiled as he sipped the beer. "Just have to practice moderation, especially when it comes to liquor. Wish I could find a little cupcake moderation," he laughed, patting his oversized gut.

Caleb found himself telling Pastor Dan his life story, the big man nodding and congratulating him on anything that resembled an accomplishment. He'd never been around anyone so confident and positive. And the next Sunday Caleb was in the last place he'd ever expected to be—church. He had, in fact, been looking forward to it all week, yearning to be in Pastor Dan's sphere.

News of the preacher spread fast, most scoffing at first, but the church began to fill. It started with the old folks, anxious for any house of God they wouldn't have to drive more than a couple miles to frequent, but then the entertainment-starved began to show up. Pastor Dan's three ring circus, the place to be on Sundays. Sometimes he'd blast Earth, Wind, & Fire, dancing the parishioners down the aisle to their seats.

He had the choral group from Stevenson High come sing Christmas carols. Set up Bible study for the kids. Served coffee cake after every service, and spaghetti dinners the third Tuesday of the month; free food being a big draw in Carson. He sponsored a Boy Scout troupe. A pediatrician from Portland lectured on child nutrition. A guy from Sterling Bank gave a talk on how to get out of debt. Thursday nights he screened movies in the church, not Jesus-y movies, but feel good films. *Field of Dreams, A River Runs Through It*. Within a few months, The Carson Bible Church drew a crowd, parishioners forgetting Pastor Dan looked nothing like them. And after a year or so, when he started to channel Jesus, everyone took it in stride, many believing, others figuring it just part of the show. But a good part.

Then came recruiting. "Time to spread the word," Pastor Dan told the congregation. He broke the willing into two-person teams. "Knock on those doors for Jesus." He armed everyone with flyers: The Carson Bible Church Invites You to Join Our Community. Not heavy religious propaganda, just a pitch for neighbors meeting neighbors.

Caleb was paired with frumpster Mrs. Allen. The two began canvassing homes every Sunday after services. Mrs. Allen, though only in her mid-thirties, looked as if she'd been transported from 1953 after raiding her grandmother's closet, her tiny body hidden in heavy, dark tweed clothing, even on the steamiest days. Always under some kind of hat. She didn't watch television and called computers and cell phones "devilish distractions." No interest in news or culture, or anything occurring further out than thirty miles.

Caleb once jokingly called the two of them Cagney and Lacey, a reference so old he figured she'd get it, but she stared at him as if he'd spoken Swahili. Still, she provided some decent companionship, and Caleb sensed a big heart under all that wool.

So as to not appear Mormon or Jehovah, Caleb wore black Lee's, his best western shirt, and his cleanest Century Link cap. Still, most people have an aversion to anyone knocking uninvited. A few times they were chased off by men brandishing firearms. "You're goddamn crazy if you think I'd go to that nigger church," screamed one old redneck.

It was a game of odds. Knock enough and you'll be invited in. They spent a lot of time with the old and lonely, sipping Nescafe in tiny kitchens that smelled of mildewing linoleum, hallways lined with forty-year-old photos of the lingering dead. Those were the simple converts. Often, Mrs. Allen would have to pick up the old folks to get them to the church, as their drivers licenses expired during the Reagan administration. Others sporting big holes in their lives were easy marks. Divorce, addictions, loss of loved ones, jobs, or self-respect, they just wanted to tell their story and receive a little acknowledgement as opposed to judgment. The valley was pocketed with loneliness, and to them he and Mrs. Allen were a kind of salvation. It gave Caleb a reason to go knocking. Plus, he figured this was good training. In all his motivational books, the authors had a story about the low-level job that propelled them to success. Maybe ringing doorbells for Jesus would be his turning point. And it drew the attention of Pastor Dan, something Caleb really craved.

He spent more and more time at the church, doing handyman work and running errands. He and Pastor Dan sat on the front steps, drinking Snapple, or sometimes a beer, and eating bologna sandwiches, Caleb soliciting advice, hanging on every word, sucking up any warmth Pastor Dan offered. "Caleb, you've got talent," Dan garbled with a full mouth. "You're putting yourself in a fine position for this life, and the afterlife." Caleb's heart leaped.

One afternoon, Caleb and Mrs. Allen were knocking on doors at homes near Wind River Highway when they drove by the big house. It sat on twenty fenced acres, gated in sculptured steel with discreet cameras ringing the property. Caleb knew the place. A year earlier during construction he'd been called out to hook up the internet and phone lines. He'd never seen anything like it except in movies. Acres of gardens and ponds, a tennis court and a swimming pool, a six-car garage. Small-town rumors abounded as to the owners: doctors, drug dealers, mobsters; nobody knew for sure, but the consensus in a poor town is that nobody gets rich by being honest.

Caleb had seen the owners at The Mart a couple times; movie-star handsome in fine clothes, a glossy Mercedes SUV with a proud Golden Retriever perched in the rear compartment. He wondered what it was like to be them, driving around in fancy cars that cushion you from every bump and smell. Eating food that didn't arrive wrapped in paper.

What was it like to be that man? Crawling under clean soft sheets with a woman that smelled fresh? A woman you never needed to check for ticks. One that wore new underwear and never flew into unexplainable rages, vomited in your sink, or took a baseball bat to your truck.

And this woman! Lemon-lit shoulder-length hair that looked just-washed. Thirty-five, maybe even forty, but perfect, the slim body of a college girl, a fine high ass curving out jeans that probably cost a truck payment. Caleb envisioned her in tight yoga clothes on that big deck overlooking the river as she stretched every which way.

"Let's try there," he said to Mrs. Allen, motioning at the gate.

She frowned. "Those kinda' folks don't want to hear anything we have to say."

Caleb pulled into the driveway and hit the gate button. "Rich folks got to know Jesus too. Might even need him more."

There was a metallic tone, a few clicks, and then a woman with a thick accent answered. "Yasss? Can I halp you?"

Caleb stared into the tiny camera lens below the button. "Afternoon, we're with The Carson Bible Church, and we wanted to drop off a little information on what we've got going on. Would love to talk to you about all the great events we're having."

"Thaaank yooou, but de owners not here. You can put information in mailbox or come back."

Come back. Caleb took that as a positive. An invitation, really.

Three days later, he returned to the house by himself, surprised to see the gate open, two flatbed trucks unloading plants and fertilizer. He drove into the roundabout, and approached a group of men he assumed to be gardeners. But when one of them turned he recognized him as the owner, covered in dirt, wearing rubber boots, work gloves, and a G. Loomis baseball cap.

"What can I do for you," his tone unexpectedly friendly.

Caleb introduced himself, and mentioned he'd stopped by on Sunday to drop off some information and had been told to come back.

"Is that the church just past downtown?" the man asked with real curiosity. "I'd wondered about that place. A lot of cars around there the last few months. Do you work there?"

"No, just a volunteer." Caleb explained that he was employed by Century Link, and had actually worked on the house when it was being built.

The man looked at Caleb with renewed curiosity. "Century Link. You know about routers?"

"Sure."

The man smiled with relief. "Terrific. Tell you what. Come in and see if you can get my internet working. It went down last night, and I really need to get a few things out. I'll treat you to a beer, and you tell me all about your church. I'll pay you too. Sound good?"

Caleb nodded, believing there was some real divine intervention going on here.

The man stripped a glove and extended a hand. "I'm Peter." He led him up the ornate path to a massive hammered metal door, ten feet tall, mounted on heavy iron pinions.

Inside, Peter led him through a glass walled room into a stone and stainless steel kitchen bigger than Caleb's entire house. It overlooked a bend of the river that backed up to the Gifford Pinchot Forest. It was the biggest room Caleb had ever seen in a house. More like the lobby at Skamania Lodge. The floors were exotic wood, the walls covered in expensive-looking native art, intricately carved paddles, screaming masks, flowing feather headdresses.

Then she came around the corner.

"Peter, you found a new friend?"

Caleb flinched at the sight of her. She was barefoot, slim copper legs disappearing into khaki shorts, a simple white linen shirt that seemed to have been sewn around her. Her eyes, shiny bright aquamarine, like a beautiful alien. Caleb envisioned putting his hands around her waist and spinning her around like a couple in a Pepsi commercial.

Peter removed two pale ales from the fridge, a brand Caleb admired but could not afford. He popped the tops with a fancy pewter opener and handed Caleb the beer. "Suzy, this is Caleb. Apparently God sent him down to save us in our internet moment of need."

"Thank God," she said sarcastically. "Caleb, I'm afraid maybe my husband blew up the system last night. Too much porno or Downton Abbey. Not sure which."

"No talk of porno," Peter said. "Caleb actually stopped by to drop off some literature on the church in town before I hijacked him. We wouldn't want the nice folks of Carson thinking we're a bunch of sinning heathens."

"Heathens," Caleb snorted happily. He loved how rich people talked.

Peter led him through a series of art-covered hallways that wound through the house and ended at a temperature controlled room lined with racks of stereo and security equipment, lighting and climate control systems. Sitting at the intersection of everything was the burnt-out router. Caleb proclaimed it dead and replaced it with one he found in his truck. Anxious to impress Peter, he also made a variety of suggestions on how to speed up his internet and clean-up some wiring issues.

Thrilled to have the system working, Peter pulled a hundred-dollar bill, and three twenties from his wallet, slid them into Caleb's shirt pocket, then invited him to join them for another drink on the deck. Caleb couldn't remember ever having a hundred-dollar bill, and thought he could somehow feel the weight of it against his chest.

It was like hanging out with Brad and Angelina. They sank down on thick cushions in low-slung furniture. Caleb's deck was a cracked concrete slap, permanently blood-stained in the corner where his Dad used to dress deer after hunting. His patio furniture consisted of three old metal chairs he'd found sitting next to a dumpster, polyester ticking splaying out of the cracked plastic seats. They sat poolside, Caleb marveling at his blue-toned reflection. Not like the places he swam, local rivers and lakes, which were clean enough, but mushroomed brown as you walked, something always floating by that needed to be dodged.

"Okay, fair is fair. You handled your part of the bargain. Tell us about your church." Peter picked up the brochure Caleb had set down.

He did the abbreviated pitch, trying to figure out what it was that might be of interest to people like this. "Sounds great, but we're not much for religion," Suzy said. "We do like to support the community, so if there's something we can do, maybe contribute to a fund raiser, we'd be happy to help." She reached down to stroke the dog that had planted himself at her feet. A perfect dog, not like the smelly, frantic animals Caleb knew that were always yapping and farting. Even rich people's dogs were different.

Caleb asked to use a restroom, and they directed him down the hall. "Third door, right past the laundry," Suzy pointed. Walking past the laundry he ducked his head into the open door. Fancy German stainless-steel appliances were flanked by bright white cabinets. Suzy's clean lingerie had been folded and set on the counter like colorful little presents. Caleb fingered one of her sheer bras, noting the ornate French label. He picked up a pair of her panties, a tiny tangerine silk he suspected was as soft as her skin. In the bathroom, he marveled at the French soap, and coated his hands with the cream that smelled of burnt lemon.

Returning to his seat, Caleb peeled at the label on his bottle, thinking Pastor Dan would want him to take one more shot. "Can I ask; do you believe in God?"

"No idea," Suzy replied. "Maybe. I suspect if she does exist she isn't at all like men make her out to be. God wouldn't live in a big building and insist people worship her, or donate all their money just to please her. God wouldn't get involved in politics or discriminate against people."

God's a she! Caleb loved how self-confident Suzy was. Heck, maybe God was a woman. When Suzy leaned back, her shirt hiked-up and he could see an inch of her flat belly. He tried not to be obvious, pretending he was looking at a trio of hummingbirds hovering on a flowering bush, and quickly scanned her legs for any sign of a tattoo. Nothing. Not like the girls in Carson who covered their bodies in ink, paragraphs of silly faux Asian wisdom ringing their waists, stretched eagles and entire rose gardens spread over their skin like circus performers.

Feeling more comfortable now, he thought about what Dale Carnegie would do in this situation. "Peter, hope you don't mind me asking, but what do you do for a living? Whatever it is, you're obviously very good at it."

Peter smiled and rose. "Come with me."

He led him to the pantry behind the kitchen and slid open a long drawer that held a plastic spice rack. At first Caleb thought he was going to show him oregano or dill, maybe he was some kind of spice importer, but he pulled out a tall pill bottle—The Green Miracle— and set it in front of Caleb. "Know what this is?"

In Carson, smoking marijuana was a fifth grade rite of passage, and Caleb certainly enjoyed a little weed now and then. "Looks like some primo pot."

"The best. The Green Miracle. Don't be concerned. It's all legal. I'm a botanist by training, and we grow medical marijuana for clinics all through the West. Suzy's a lawyer and handles the business part. Course I'm biased, but The Green Miracle is as good as it gets." He motioned at the different vials in the rack. "These are my babies. We grow sleepy time Green Miracle, Green Miracle that gives you energy and makes you creative. There's a strain for almost everybody." He handed Caleb the vial. "Here, a little gift for you."

Caleb's eyes grew wide. So they are drug dealers.

Peter laughed. "Don't freak out. We're not breaking any laws. Perfectly legit. As I'm sure you know, it's legal in Washington, Oregon, and Colorado now. We're in a big expansion mode. Opening up retail stores. I guess like everyone else we want to be the Starbucks of marijuana."

Caleb popped the top of his vial and sniffed the rich aroma. Nothing like the skunk weed he grew up smoking.

"Caleb, I don't know how you feel about this kind of thing, but we're hiring, and we especially want people from the community. A guy like you might be perfect. I suspect a lot of your friends smoke pot. We're opening a shop in Stevenson, and you might make a great manager. Heck, if you've got the self-confidence to go door-to-door selling religion, you'd do well at The Green Miracle. My guess is we pay a lot better than Century Link. Interested?"

Caleb nodded, wondering how his mom would feel about him going into the drug business. Still, maybe this was divine intervention. Heck, booze was illegal once, but there was certainly no shame selling it now. Maybe it would be the same with pot, but Caleb would be in on the ground floor. He'd heard a lot of rich guys started as bootleggers.

"Wow, Peter, that's a really nice offer. I'd have to think about it, but out of curiosity, what kind of money does a manager make?"

"That depends on how good you are. Base salary starts at about sixty thousand, but you get performance bonuses. Most of my manager's make anywhere from seventy-five K to as much as a hundred and a quarter."

Caleb paused. "A hundred and twenty-five thousand dollars?"

Peter nodded, went into the kitchen, reached into a briefcase, and pulled out a booklet, "Welcome to The Green Miracle Team" emblazoned on the cover. "Take a look at this. It describes the company. The requirements and rules. If you're interested and can meet the qualifications, drop me an email. I put my card in there. I'd be happy to line-up an interview."

Caleb said his goodbyes and climbed into his truck. Driving through town he stopped at the church. He could hear the thumping baseline of Stevie Wonder's "Superstition" as he approached the building. Pastor Dan, sweat-soaked, sans jacket but wearing bright ochre suit pants and a matching vest, was leading a conga line of women down the aisle, wiping his glossy head with a handkerchief, knees raised in high-step as if stomping out a fire. He twirled and clapped to the rhythm, eyes shut tight. Behind him, the Widow Davis, contorting in ways Caleb wouldn't have thought possible for an eighty-three-year-old. And shock of shocks, behind her, Mrs. Allen, clapping and howling. She'd stripped off the heavy jacket, and though still clad in a thick wool skirt and sweater, for the first time Caleb could see she actually had limbs. Two other gray-haired women were behind them, clapping, laughing, and occasionally twirling each other in a stilted white woman's ballet.

"Ladies. Good news, looks like we have a dancing partner." Pastor Dan smiled, motioning for Caleb to join them. "C'mon Caleb, we got a little Master Blaster coming up. Shake your thing."

Caleb had never really been comfortable on a dance floor, but knew from experience there was no arguing with Pastor Dan. He moved toward the group, looking more like a man riding an invisible horse than a dancer, finally finding a groove. Mrs. Allen gave him a playful poke and a hip bump. "Can I talk to you when you're done?" he shouted at Dan.

Later, the two cooled off on the front steps, Caleb relating his adventures with the rich folks. After Caleb described the house, he got to the real issue and explained the job offer. "How would Jesus feel about a guy selling pot?"

Pastor Dan laughed. "Caleb, I might channel God's son every now and then, but I don't know his opinion on that kind of thing. I suspect he prefers our minds' clear and bodies' healthy, but I also know he enjoyed a little wine now and then. Life's stressful, and a little natural help relaxing isn't a bad idea. He created weed, so he must have had some kind of plan.

As I've told you, it's all about moderation. I guess the question is how you'd feel about it? Is it against your moral code? Cause if it is, you shouldn't do it. Would it change your relationship with your mother and your friends? On the other hand, it's legal, and it could be a good opportunity. So follow your heart. Long as you do, and your heart is good, which I know yours is, the Lord will back you up." Pastor Dan reached up to give Caleb a half hug. "Now my curiosity is killing me. Pull out a little of that bud so I can take a sniff. I'm dying to know what high grade marijuana smells like."

Caleb ended up splitting his Green Miracle with Dan, promising not to mention it to anyone. "You know, sometimes I get these back aches, and I hear a little puff can be very therapeutic," Dan explained.

Caleb helped with a couple chores around the church, then made his way home. He was pleased to find the house empty, and headed to his room. Falling back onto his bed, he began to read the Green Miracle manual, which really wasn't all that different from the Century Link manual. Pot was officially corporate. Bored after the first two pages, he put the book down on top of the other "instruction manual" he'd been attempting to read, a Bible Pastor Dan had given him for his birthday.

Reaching into his jacket pocket, he pulled out the two "presents" he'd brought home from the fancy house. Popping the top on The Green Miracle canister, he pulled a tacky bud from the container, waving it by his nostrils to sample the sharp aroma. Next, he fingered the tiny panties he's slipped into his pocket before leaving the laundry room, confident that a woman with so much underwear wouldn't miss them. He brushed the g-string across his upper lip, marveling at the softness, inhaling the clean tang of soap and fabric softener, and perhaps just the faintest hint of her? Caleb smiled and fell back on his pillow, wondering if this was the sweet smell of success.

THE BIG CHOCOLATE WHIZZLE

LEN WILLIAMS HAD SPENT a lifetime cavorting with substance abusers, raised in a family where hitting bottom was more a rite of passage than any sign of urgent personal issues. His father's Ivy League law degree had been washed away in a fizzy river of scotch and soda. Dad now spent his rare sober hours festooned in a faded red polo shirt, hawking file cabinets at Staples. Mom's annual vacation destination—Hazleton Rehab Center—where she recovered from her latest foray with cocaine derivations and prescription pain killers. Usually consumed while pursuing her love of gambling.

Sister Kate, young enough to be a hot mess, as opposed to just the mess that seemed inevitable, was drawn to obsessions of the flesh: sex addiction, bulimia, excessive love of tattoo needles, and an occasional bloody cutting fetish when a relationship blew apart. Aunt Shelly's compulsions centered on the edible, an oral fixation that at almost five hundred pounds left her unable to walk; her rhino frame tethered to a Hummer-sized electric scooter.

Len was more of a generalist when it came to his addictions, driven to pursue any unhealthy opportunity that might present itself. Pills, booze, a wide range of snort able substances, inebriated sexual encounters that reeked of vomit and danger, his preference was to remain stoned and oblivious to the consequences any adventure might produce.

Like the morning after the 2008 Presidential election, when he awoke in a chunky puddle of cranberry vodka vomit. Initially hoping the red mess didn't signify some kind of hemorrhage, he was horrified to discover something even more disturbing as he traced the stinging pain on his backside; Nancy Pelosi's coiffed face tattooed on his left butt cheek. It was the payoff for a Cape Cod-induced wager with coworkers that his favorite Texan would easily defeat the "Muslim smart-ass."

Then there was the night ex-wife number two had Len arrested as he pranced naked in front of her condo, executing a plan concocted during happy hour at The Martini Ranch—SADDLE UP FOR THE WORLD'S BIGGEST MARTINIS.

"Bitch! Take my clothes. Take my money. Take my goddamn hair. You've taken everything else!" he screamed. His clothes heaped on the lawn, he hacked at his thinning yellow locks with garden shears while kicking the back of her eight-year-old Saab. His terrified eight-year-old daughter watched from the second story window as the police shoved her naked father headfirst into to the back of a cruiser.

Of course, this was not Len's first encounter with the authorities. He'd long ago lost his legal right to operate a motor vehicle and spent more than one night huddled on a steel cot, knees pulled tight. He'd watch nervously as dangerous men zombie-walked the drunk tank, glancing at Len with dead eyes, sizing him up for a beating, or something more intimate.

But none of his previous antics had prepared Len for the situation he now found himself in. After boarding Alaska Airlines Flight 71 from LA to Portland, he downed three gin and tonics to chase down the mysterious pink pills he'd discovered in his shirt pocket. Maybe Maalox, but hopefully budget Mexican Vicodin from the last trip to Cabo, and at 33,000 feet he was in trouble. Len had a keen sense of injustice (or his "silly persecution complex", as wife number two called it) which always intensified when he was under the influence. As he stared at the curtain separating First Class from Coach, he was suddenly struck by the unfairness of it all; Alaska Airlines own Iron Curtain, separating the haves from the have not's.

"What gives them the right?" He turned to his seat mate. "We're as good as anyone on the other side of that curtain. Probably better because we actually work for a living." The young woman, already suffering from a fear of flying, nodded frantically and scanned the aisle for safe haven. "Did you see those assholes when we boarded, sipping Bloody Marys' while the rest of us peons shuffled to the back of the bus? Well fuck them, and fuck this airline." He punctuated his points by pounding the seat in front of him, eliciting an angry stare as the offended passenger swiveled to peer through the seats.

But Len had clarity. This was his moment. His time to lead and do something important. He suddenly saw himself the Martin Luther King of the skies, a flying Gandhi, really. Pushing aside his terrified seatmate, he jumped into the aisle. "We want free cocktails and complimentary cashews," he yelled at the baffled group. "We deserve more than plastic shit," reaching to grab a Dixie cup out of a passenger's hands, then flinging it to the floor and stomping on it. "C'mon, let's tear down that curtain!"

He waited a beat, surprised his fellow travelers didn't offer encouragement. Most looked stunned, one yelling, "Sit down asshole," as a flight attendant scurried toward him. "Sir, please, be seated," she yelled.

Len felt disoriented, then regained his focus. He sprinted toward the curtain, tossing a male flight attendant across several shocked laps and sending cups flying. Barging into First Class, he hollered, "We belong up here too." Spying a heavy aluminum service cart in the aisle, he saw his chance to make the ultimate statement on behalf of the people. If "the man" was going to treat the average guy like shit, then he would return the favor. Crawling on the shaky platform, and perched like someone mounting a surf board for the first time, he dropped his baggy suit pants and boxers, and was now attempting to defecate on the plates of hot cookies the flight attendant had just prepared.

"How do you like this, you rich bastards," he screamed, gin spittle flying, as the shocked passengers recoiled. "Let me add a little fudge to your fancy cookies."

Before he could finish frosting the desserts, two oversized Nike sales representatives grabbed him off the cart, flinging him six feet through the air into the galley. They'd been looking forward to dessert for the last twenty minutes, and weren't gentle in their approach. As they held him down, three irate flight attendants and the copilot handcuffed Len to the toilet. The steward Len assaulted took special care to position him so his head hovered inches above the pungent toilet bowl.

"Here you go asshole," he whispered in Len's ear as he flushed, shoving his face into the acidic blue water designed to eradicate even the most threatening microbe. The Federal Marshalls who removed Len from the plane in Portland were shocked to discover a pants-less prisoner who resembled a cast member from Blue Man Group.

This was a difficult situation to explain, but as he stood in court Len tried to dampen the seriousness of his offense. "I think it was a combination of the one cocktail and a Benadryl I took for my allergies. Wacked me out. I'd never normally do something so crazy. Probably the altitude too. I'm sensitive to heights."

The judge was unimpressed, and given Len's history sentenced him to two years in prison. "The people that cleaned the plane had to wear hazmat suits, you idiot. Lucky I don't send you to Guantanamo for being a terrorist."

Len lost his job at Verizon, and both his ex-wives petitioned to keep him away from his kids. The flight attendant won a $150,000 civil judgment, claiming he now suffered from fibromyalgia. Len didn't have that kind of money, so they drained his bank account and auctioned off his nine-year-old Miata.

He did gain a lot of notoriety from the incident. Every major news network followed the case. The cast of *Fox and Friends* discussed him at length, concluding "alcoholism and mental illness is very sad, and perhaps we need more armed air marshals to prevent this kind of thing."

An online T-shirt company developed a cartoonish image of Len, sans pants, propped over a plate of desserts, maniacal smile on his face, with the headline, "HERE'S SOME FUDGE FOR YOUR FANCY LITTLE COOKIES," which became a common mantra across high school and college campuses for several weeks.

Saturday Night Live recreated the event in a music video that gained enormous viral popularity called "Pooping on a Plane," featuring Andy Samberg as the flight attendant and Justin Timberlake in a blonde wig as Len. Although the iTunes version was downloaded over 180,000 times, Len didn't receive a dime.

Vanity Fair did an in-depth profile, but much to his dismay they called him a "chronic alcoholic loser with an acute personality disorder." He thought about selling his life story for a book, but his attorney advised that since he still owed the flight attendant $144,000, any profits would be garnished, and he seriously doubted there would be much of a market anyway.

And maybe because this time he really had hit rock bottom, Len decided use his prison experience to reshape his life. He joined the prison ministry, Cons for Christ. He earned an Associate Degree in iPad repair from DeVry University's Felon Education Program, and put his former sales experience to good use, working part-time in the prison's telemarketing center, taking orders for the Sundance Catalog. Twice, he won the "salesperson of the month award," for which he received a pair of Robert Redford red agate cufflinks and a leather vest with a blue buffalo embossed on the back.

At the suggestion of his cell mate Nicky Belmont, an amiable arsonist from Caldwell, Idaho, he signed up for menbehindbars.com, a dating site where the incarcerated could meet the kind of women that sought out bad boys. He corresponded with several romantic candidates, but found there was something about his particular crime that turned them off. "It's one thing to tell someone your boyfriend is in prison because he's in a biker gang and was caught dealing meth or setting an African American church on fire," Becky from Woodland, Washington explained, "but when you say I'm dating the guy that went to jail because he shit on a tray of cookies, people don't respect you."

Finally, on a rainy December day, Len was paroled to begin what he hoped would be a wonderful new chapter in his life. He felt good about all he'd done to rehabilitate himself. Perhaps I'll meet a nice Christian woman, he fantasized. We'll marry and have a couple kids. And this time, I'll be a good father. Len visualized himself coaching Little League, or sitting in a darkened arena watching his daughter's dance recital. He dreamt of getting a job at one of those shiny Apple stores he'd been reading about.

At his release, they gave him new Kirkland-brand jeans, a bright white shirt and tennis shoes, and $980 he'd earned over the last two years working for Sundance. As he inspected himself in the mirror, he took the white shirt and shoes as a sign from God, noting that he'd now perfectly compliment an all-white Apple store, a place that must have been designed with heaven in mind. And he finally had the opportunity to don his beautiful Sundance leather vest and cufflinks, poking extra holes into the cuffs on the shirt with a scissors so he could wear his Robert Redford's. To protect the vest from the rain, the guards gave him a black garbage bag, and he cut a hole through the top to fashion into a poncho.

Len walked two miles to the nearest town, hoping to find a bus to San Francisco where he assumed there would be a plethora of iPad-repair opportunities. By the time he hit the city limits the rain had stopped, so he pulled off the garbage bag and gave it to a homeless man he found dumpster-diving in a park. "Thanks man, but how about that vest? The blue buffalo is really trippy." Len smiled and handed the guy a five from his stash, a down payment on the virtuous life he now intended to lead. "Hey," the guy yelled after him, "I don't suppose you'd take five dollars for that vest?"

He found an Applebee's in the city center, and decided to celebrate his release with a good meal. Len perused the menu, choosing the early-bird special; the steak, ribs, and shrimp combo for $15.99. "Anything to drink with that?" For a second Len was frozen by the perky waitress, the only woman he'd seen in months, noting her high ass and flawless skin. He breathed hard, unaccustomed to being served by someone who wasn't wearing a paper hat and a two-day beard, and glanced around. Applebee's was such a friendly place. Perfect for his first meal as a free man. Neon signs over the bar. Funny slogans burned into wood plaques on the walls. Corny, but the real America. He envisioned sitting in an Applebee's with his wife and kids, living the American dream.

He inspected his table. There was tented card perched near the napkin holder advertising the drink specials of the week. Probably wouldn't hurt to have some kind of cocktail. I do have a good reason to celebrate, and nobody is more sober than me after two years without a drop, he reasoned as he ordered a special Long Island ice tea called The New York Fishbowl. He smiled widely at the patrons being seated, nodding and mouthing "Hi-ya," and "Afternoon." Prison taught patience, and he was overjoyed to be around normal people. He rubbed his hands up and down the smooth shellacked table.

His drink, sad-looking fruit slices floating on top of a cloudy brown punch, arrived in an actual tiny aquarium designed to be shared by two or even three people. Len sucked the sweet liquid hard through a long straw, the slight liquor burn at the back of his throat conjuring up forgotten emotions.

He analyzed a poster on the wall advertising The Big Chocolate Whizzle, some kind of ice cream concoction that looked delicious, yet somehow disgusting. He felt a little chill as the liquor took hold, followed by a familiar buzz at the base of his spine. Glancing around at the Applebee's' patrons, he suddenly noted how many were grossly overweight, polyester-clad asses hanging over wide wooden chairs. In his sight-line there were three or four big folks shoveling in French fries and sandwiches slathered in barbecue sauce and mayonnaise. He stared at a Kenworth-sized man, remnants of his meal trailing in his beard.

In prison, with plenty of time to work out every day, Len had trimmed down, and he was proud of his new svelte form and thick, defined guns. He'd come to realize that part of his problem had been his own lack of self-respect, which had been a reflection of how he treated his own body. But these people… They shouldn't be eating all this fatty food. Certainly not anything called The Big Chocolate Whizzle. They were Applebee's addicts, slaves to this high caloric crap that imprisoned them in big bodies and killed them off with diabetes. Another example of "the man" putting one over on the little people. Len felt a rising irritation.

When dinner arrived he forgot his concerns and tore into his meal, washing it down with another New York Fishbowl. Thirty minutes later as he drained his third cocktail, Len could feel his bowels rumbling.

Not used to all this rich food, he thought as he glanced around, tension growing in his stomach. He began to see Applebee's for what it really was, another faceless corporation that manipulated the working man, Len suddenly flooded by his old sense of injustice. He could feel himself being transported to that place, a place he hadn't visited for a long time, often a bad place, but one he somehow missed.

Fucking Applebee's. He looked up in disgust at the signs on the wall. "Screw you," he said under his breath. "I will not wear a happy face, and I sure as hell don't brake for brownies!" He focused on a table six feet away, four teenagers eating burgers. Most of the folks in this place were beyond redemption. They'd accepted the Applebee's way of life. But perhaps he could save the young.

"Don't do it kids," he yelled at them. "Don't eat that shitty food. Don't give into Applebee's. If you do, one day you'll wake-up fat and broke. Your wife will divorce you and take your kids and money. You'll probably end up working here in the kitchen, scraping other people's plates," he screamed, rising from his booth. His fellow diners watched in alarm, pulling their children closer. His waitress moved toward him, then recoiled as he grew more menacing.

"And nobody should eat anything called The Big Chocolate Whizzle," he shouted, raising the empty aquarium over his head and smashing it into the poster. The crowd dropped beneath their tables to avoid flying glass. Lemon and lime slices stuck to the surface, then slid to the ground leaving a snail-like brown trail. Suddenly Len saw something eerily familiar, as he eyed a big rolling dessert cart designed to make custom ice cream sundaes.

Perfect.

"Hey, how about if I give Applebee's a little present...my own little chocolate Whizzle," he screamed, gut rumbling, as he tugged as his belt and sprinted toward the cart.

THE PURIFICATION

Dewey jumped at the interruption, then glanced in annoyance at the thin head framed in the doorway. The clatter of boots on the wooden sidewalk or the loud whining of handcuffed drunks normally served as an angry knock. He wasn't accustomed to youngsters visiting his office.

He'd been immersed in the new Sears catalog, fingering the bedding section with careful consideration as he imagined plopping his head on thick feather pillows. Thirty-nine cents each. Not cheap, but any relief to his sore neck ever since his horse spooked would be worth the purchase. He'd been riding near Greenough Lake, investigating Tommy Dillon's report of a bad-tempered grizzly absconding with his brother while they were poaching deer. Tommy had barged into Dewey's office, bloody and bruised and looking like he'd rolled down the canyon, spouting a wild tale about a psychotic bear that knocked them down. Said the animal ripped off one of his brother's arms, and dragged the body by its gushing neck into the ravine. Tommy, not the bravest man in Carbon County, had hightailed it out, figuring nothing that big would be dissuaded by a Winchester 30–30.

Knowing the Dillon brothers, Dewey suspected the tale was born in the bottom of a bottle, but figured he'd take a ride out anyway. Belle wasn't normally skittish, but they'd both been surprised by the roaring form, huge and brown as a barn, exploding out of a thicket of cottonwoods. Belle reared, catapulting Dewey onto a wide-felled pine. He feared he'd look up just in time to see yellow teeth spread wide for his neck, but the animal ambled off, satisfied to create a little non-lethal carnage. Dewey felt fortunate his spine hadn't snapped. Ever since, the pain felt like he'd been wearing a ten-pound hat.

He glanced curiously at the boy, his body still hidden by the door, a top-notch of dirty red hair poking through. The kid looked at him with wide, feral eyes. "Come in, boy. What can I do you for?" Dewey puffed his smoldering cigar to life as the door swung open. The boy was slight, five two or three, but with enough sinewy muscle that Dewey knew he was slim from hard work and not from a lack of food. He guessed he was thirteen or fourteen, dressed in a stained white shirt and the rough woolen trousers favored by the Mennonites. His boots and pants were splattered with sandy red mud, indicating the boy had taken back roads and not the cobblestoned main street. His right cheek mushroomed angry purple, blood crusted near his ear lobe, like someone had taken a two-by-four to the side of his head.

He looked at the floor nervously, one hand picking at the other as if he intended to rip skin from a knuckle. "Uh, Sheriff, I'm surely sorry to bother you, but I got no other place to go, and I was hoping maybe you could maybe lock me up."

"Lock you up? You do something wrong?" The kid looked familiar, but there was something odd about him. Not necessarily in a bad way, but he had a sheen. Aside from the bruise, he could be an actor from the movie theater that had just opened up the street. More beautiful than handsome, a face that would be equally pleasant on a man or woman.

"Not sure I did anything wrong, but my pa seems to think so. He took after me yesterday. Beat me hard. He does that sometimes, but not like yesterday. He aimed to kill me and drop my body down one of those old mine shafts up Rock Creek. Send me to hell, he said, and I tend to believe he means it. He tripped while he was going for an axe, and I ran out. Otherwise, I'm pretty sure he'd have chopped my head off. I spent the night in the woods, but I can't survive out there by myself. Not for long anyway, so I came to town. I got nothing to pay my way, but Pa said the Sheriff was hired to protect folks."

"Why in the world would your Pa want to cut your head off?" Dewey frowned, blowing a billowy line of smoke, thinking he probably knew the answer. The hills around Red Lodge were chock-full of angry men: dust-covered miners working worthless claims, drunks cutting a little timber to support shiftless lives, reprobates and crazies that enjoyed taking their frustrations out on the women and children that sometimes wandered into their lives.

The boy seemed embarrassed. "He says I'm wrong in the head. There's evil in me. That I'm a tempter and a pox. Said Satan sent me down to confuse men and drag them off to hell, and by killing me he'd help save mankind."

Dewey tapped an ash and snorted in disgust. "Who might your father be?"

"Canner Shultz." The boy announced the name as if introducing a political candidate. "He works a claim near Soda Butte. You might know him. He sure knows you. Told me you killed Lester Andrews and his brother. Called you a real old-time gunfighter, like Wyatt Earp." The boy brightened at the mention. It amazed Dewey, the different ways an old story could be retold.

Canner Shultz. Not a name Dewey cared to hear, but it made sense. He now remembered seeing the kid in town with Canner and his wife two, three years earlier, the boy just a pipsqueak. He'd heard that the boy's mom had since died with her second in childbirth.

Canner arrived in Red Lodge representing himself as a preacher, spouting his own brand of angry religion, which folks found anything but comforting. In fact, Canner's God seemed a sadistic son-of-a-bitch. Somehow he'd met a woman; Dewey recalled she was from Bridger, and after they married he gave up the Jesus business and moved out of town to strike it rich mining.

After his wife passed, Canner sometimes came to Red Lodge, mumbling to Jesus, as if tragedy afforded him a direct line to the

Lord. Apparently, Jesus told him to drink, as he was known to tear up a saloon from time to time. In fact, he'd spent more than one night in this very building, sleeping it off behind bars. Whenever Canner got out of control, Dewey knew to send at least two deputies and avoid the scene himself, feeling too old these days to engage in barroom antics, especially with a man of Canner's dimensions and disposition.

The boy had inherited Canner's red hair and long Germanic nose, but not yet his size. Dewey himself was a big man, 6'2" and stout, but Canner towered over him, probably 6'5", tree trunk legs, and knotted arms hardened by years of sluicing. Dewey wasn't inclined toward fear, but he always approached Canner with caution.

He peered at the youngster as he moved into the room and raised a hand toward the boy's chin, who recoiled, then moved forward when he understood Dewey meant no harm. "Nasty bruise," Dewey said, turning the boy's head, examining the red rivulet below his right ear. "Can you hear okay?"

The boy nodded. "Yeah, it's sore, but I hear fine."

"You hurt anywhere else?"

The boy blew a long sigh, shaking his head an unconvincing no. "Does this mean you'll lock me up?"

"This isn't a hotel. The jail is for criminals, and you don't appear to be breaking any laws. Now your Pa; that might be a different matter." Dewey traced a bruise that began at the base of the boy's skull and disappeared somewhere south of his collar bone.

"You can't go after my pa. You do that and he really will kill me. I don't want to get him in no trouble, I just don't want him to catch me. I can sleep anywhere, and I can help out. I'm good at cleaning," the boy said, motioning at the wood stove, "I could keep the stove stoked. I make fine coffee too. Even cook a bit. Not fancy, but Pa likes it. I won't be any trouble, and soon as I figure out how to make some money, I'll be on my way. Maybe get a job over in Billings. I'm mighty strong for my size."

He winced when Dewey's hand dropped to his shoulder. "Son, take your shirt off."

The boy shook his head, moving toward the door. "Probably I shouldn't be here. I don't want no trouble."

"Take your shirt off," Dewey said firmly, then fought back a gulp when he saw the boy's naked torso, the rope-like scars on his stomach and across his back, some healed clean, but others hanging bits of bloody dried skin. "Good God, what did he do to you?"

"He purifies me sometimes," the boy said in a whisper.

"What do you mean, purifies?"

"He gets drunk, ties me up, and brands me with the fire pokin' rods. Sometimes I pass out. Claims they're signs to rid me of Satan. Cleanse me of the sin that lives in me. But last night he said it was too late, that the Devil had me for good."

"Jesus Christ. Did he do this anywhere else on your body?"

The boy nodded. "I'm like this all over. My legs, my behind, even the top of my feet. That hurt the worst."

"Let me see."

The boy dropped his pants. He was wearing rough homemade underwear that hung to his knees, his calves and feet a mass of scars. Dewey lowered the shorts a couple inches, revealing long crosses branded into his buttocks. "How long has he been doing this?"

"It started a couple months after my Ma died. Sometimes I'd wake up, maybe because I could smell him. He smells mean. Sour. He'd be sitting on the side of my bed staring at me. He'd touch me, at first kind of soft, but then he gets angry. And then the beatings, and after a while…" The boy drifted off and traced a finger across a scar on his abdomen. "The purification."

"Christ," Dewey said, and signaled the boy to get dressed. "What's your name?"

"Jacob. Jacob Schultz. Named after my Ma's father."

Dewey gently grasped his hand, removing his finger from the scar. "Jacob, I'm going to take you to the doctor to get fixed up. We'll figure out a place for you to stay. Someplace nicer than the jail. And let me tell you something. Nobody, not your father, nobody is ever going to do anything like this to you again. Understand me? You're safe." The boy nodded, and Dewey could see how desperately he wanted to believe him.

After the incident with Belle and the bear, Dewey upgraded his mode of transportation. Bouncing on even the gentlest horse made his neck ache even worse. Surprisingly, the Carbon County Commissioners hadn't objected when he requisitioned a new 1915 Model T, the first real police car within five counties. Dewey was popular in these parts, a bridge between the violent, saloon-laden mining town that didn't want to grow up and a more progressive contingent that wanted to see Red Lodge become a real city, so the Commissioners tended to give him what he wanted.

Over the last fifteen years, Dewey had made the Carbon County Sheriff's Department into one of the best in the State of Montana. The previous year, his deputies even started wearing uniforms, all except Dewey, who preferred his Levis and Pendleton shirt. He also made sure his men were equipped with the most modern firearms, Colt 1911 automatic military pistols and Springfield pump-action 12-gauge shotguns.

Dewey had moved to Red Lodge in 1899, fresh from the Army fighting the Spaniards in Cuba. He'd come to Montana to work in the coal mines, but discovered that profession short-changed him in a couple ways, lifespan and pay, and he quickly took a job as a Sheriff's Deputy.

It was unfortunate timing. Red Lodge was out of control, ragged mean miners stumbling between twenty saloons, law enforcement content to mostly watch and help mop-up blood.

Six months into the job, Dewey's life changed. He was walking down the alley behind the Merchant's Bank when the back door burst open and a major commotion poured out. Lester Andrews and his brother Butch had been drinking for the better part of two days. When the money dried up from their tiny bit of gold, they decided to make a cash withdrawal. Not criminals, more just hardened alcoholics, Dewey normally could have taken a fist to the side of their heads and they'd have come peacefully. But Avril Thompkins, the Bank's Vice President, fired off a couple shots from the puny .22 he kept in his desk drawer.

The Brothers hadn't anticipated any resistance, and hightailed it out the back when the shooting started, Lester firing a couple times into the ceiling to slow Avril down. When he saw Dewey in the alley, he fired off another half-assed shot, the bullet whizzing five feet above his head. Dewey drew his revolver, hoping the boys would accept their predicament peacefully as he yelled, "Stop right there." But he saw a wildness in Lester's eyes that led Dewey to take aim and drop him. Butch Andrews, stumbling drunk and shocked by the smoky hole in his brother's chest, grabbed for Lester's gun, forcing Dewey to cap him too with a single shot to the forehead. No great feat of marksmanship, as both men were only five feet away, but Deputy Sheriff Dewey Mansfield still took his place in Western lore as the last gunfighter in Montana, the end of an era, the story growing more heroic with each telling.

What people didn't know was that Dewey puked into the bank's rain barrel when he saw what he'd done, and shook so badly for fifteen minutes he could barely walk. He'd never shot a man before, at least none that he knew of. Everyone he'd fired at in Cuba had been running through trees at a distance. But no matter. In the next election for Sheriff, he was a shoe-in—every town wanted a legendary gunfighter as their sheriff—a position he'd held for fifteen years. Luckily for Red Lodge, he was actually good at his job.

Jacob gasped when Dewey led him to the car. "Never been in one of these," he said, carefully sliding into the passenger seat as if it might break. His eyes widened as Dewey pulled a U-turn and headed east,

Jacob rubbing the leather dashboard with light fingertips. Cars were rare enough that people turned to stare, and Jacob waved, all smiles, as if he were the star of a parade.

Doctor McBride lived across the street from the new hospital in a white Victorian that had originally belonged to one of the Carbon Coal Company owners. "Who's your friend?" he asked when he answered the door.

"Morning, Doc. This fine young man is Jacob Schultz, and my guess is he would love one of those tasty rolls you keep around. And maybe some bacon and milk, as I don't believe he's had his breakfast yet." They led Jacob to the kitchen, and Doc put out a spread for the boy, leaving him to eat as the two men exited to the converted examination room.

"And how did young Jacob come to be here?"

"You know his old man, Canner Shultz?"

Doc nodded. "Big crazy German? Used to stand in front of the café and holler at everyone about hell and damnation?"

"That's him. I need you to examine the boy. Looks like Canner brutalized the kid pretty good. Burning, beating him, plus I fear Canner's a diddler. Never seen anything quite like it. Make you sick to your stomach. Jacob says Canner intends to kill him, and until I have a talk with the bastard, we need to keep the boy out of sight. Said he spent the night in the woods, so he'll probably sleep once he's fed and you get done looking him over. Can you put him up for a few days?"

"I'll stow him in the back bedroom."

Dewey nodded and thanked his friend. "You can update me this evening," Friday being their standing supper night.

On Tuesdays, Dewey attended the Kiwanis luncheon at The Pollard Hotel. He had no idea what Kiwanis even meant. A few of the local businessmen had opened the first charter in Montana a few months earlier, and it seemed important to spend time with the movers and shakers. Plus, it was a free lunch. As usual, Dewey was cornered by the Main Street merchants, who groused about the two whorehouses on the edge of town. Dewey suspected the men's wives made them complain, as he knew at least a couple of their husbands were patrons.

After lunch, Dewey was talking to the mayor when Dan Plummer approached. Dewey's right-hand deputy was deceptively crafty for his size and age. Most men weren't intimidated by a rotund five-foot-six-inch lawman pushing sixty, but of course, they'd never witnessed Dan's talents with the baton that swung from his belt. That morning, Dewey had told Dan to keep an eye out for Canner.

"Sorry to interrupt," Dan said, "but I wanted you to know your friend's in town. At The Lincoln, probably on his fifth beer by now."

The Mayor, always anxious for gossip, perked up. "So, there's going to be some action?"

"I doubt it," Dewey said, shaking his hand goodbye. "Just a little annoyance, is all."

Canner Schultz was sitting in the rear of the saloon, rolling a cigarette and chattering to nobody in particular. From a distance, he looked harmless enough, drunk and shaking like a man afflicted with a palsy. But as they approached, Dewey recognized the same look he saw in Lester Andrews' eyes all those years ago, right before he put a bullet in him.

"Afternoon Canner. What brings you to town?"

Canner glanced up to acknowledge Dewey. He'd lost weight, still huge, but his skin had the lemon tint of a sickly man. "Sheriff. Afternoon." He tilted his head, and said, "Come for supplies, and to look for my boy. Hoping he might've wandered into town."

Dewey nodded. "Or he might've run off, afraid for his life?" He pulled back a chair and sat down in front of Canner as Dan moved behind. "Maybe he's trying to get away from a father that beats him. A sick son-of-a-bitch that tortures him and tries to cut his head off."

Canner flashed red but stayed contained. "You know where he is?"

"Canner, child beating is against the law. Trying to kill a boy, even your own blood, that's against the law. Serious enough that you could spend the foreseeable future in Deer Lodge."

Canner snorted. "How I discipline him is my business. He's mine, and I'll do with him what I please. You just tell me where he is, for starters, and let's see what transpires from there, shall we?"

"You're not understanding the situation." Dewey leaned in. "Jacob's safe now, and you're not going to touch him. I'm this close to locking you up, maybe send you away until Jacob is full grown and might decide to take a beating to his Pa for old time's sake."

Canner rose, but Dan pushed his baton hard on his shoulder, forcing him back into his chair. "You'd do best to hold your temper," Dewey said, "Dan here senses the tiniest threat, and he'll snap your damn neck with his stick. Believe me."

Canner simmered, but stayed silent.

"You got a couple choices, "Dewey said. "You can get up, head back to your place, mind your claim, and leave the boy alone. Or you can cause trouble, and maybe we'll stop by the hospital to get you fixed-up before we lock you up. Might even forget where we put you, though I wonder who'd be seeking you out anyway. Your choice. Either works for us, given we don't care much for child beaters."

Canner slumped, rage draining. "Sheriff, you don't understand. The boy ain't right. He's got the devil in him. He's a tempter, brought here to drag men to hell. I'm just trying to do the Christian thing since I helped bring him into this world."

"There's nothing Christian about brutalizing your own blood. What's it going to be, Canner? Leave town, or we take you out of here?"

Canner thought for a moment, then lifted his hands, as if in surrender. "Alright. But remember I warned you about him. It won't be on my head." He leaned closer and dropped his voice. "Dewey, God won't forget this, and neither will I."

Dan and Dewey walked Canner to the door, watched as he mounted his horse and headed south. "This ain't the last we'll see of him," Dan said, shoving his baton into his belt. "Not sure why you didn't lock him up."

"It's a hard case," Dewey said, and slid another cigar from his pocket. "To the court, children are property. We just need to buy the boy time, keep him safe. But I agree, we haven't seen the last of Canner."

That evening, Dewey and Doc met at their usual corner table at The Red Lodge Café. Doc was already seated, and sipping what Dewey assumed was his favorite Irish whiskey. "How far ahead of me are you?" Dewey smiled as he slid into a chair.

"Sheriff, that's a complex question. You mean emotionally? Intellectually? Or are you asking if I am already half in the bag?"

"I always assume you're half in the bag," Dewey laughed. "How's our patient?"

"Never seen a boy eat and sleep like he did today. He's a sweet kid, but Christ, he's a mess. You saw the burn marks. His arm's been broke at least once. Healed off kilter a bit, but he can use it okay. Half his fingers been snapped. His left hand, it's shaped like a claw. And Canner did a lot of other serious damage that don't show. Boy's been buggered with God-knows-what. The bastard not only used the poker on his skin, but shoved it into the child's rectum. He's a mass of scars inside as well as out. Surprised he can shit. But he's tough. Accepts it like it's normal. His biggest concern is whether or not he'll get another ride in that car of yours." Doc gave Dewey a rueful smile.

Dewey shook his head in disgust. "Amazing the damage human beings inflict on each other. I've never heard of a father doing anything like that to his own son."

"The man is a psychopath and pederast of the worst kind. The boy says Canner's convinced Jacob's the devil. Religious fervor and guilt cause men do strange things. Course it certainly don't justify anything, but I suspect you see what Canner sees in Jacob? What he fears?"

"I do," Dewey nodded. "Jacob's pretty, too pretty for a boy. Confuses you just to look at him, like he's half male and half female. It's not going to make it easy. He'll draw the wrong kind of attention."

Doc sat back until the waitress finished filling his glass. "When I visit New York I see boys like Jacob, hanging around in doorways on the lower East side, sometimes working in the whorehouses, or in the new Pansy Clubs. It's a certain kind of man—a sick man—that desires a child, especially one that's neither boy nor girl. These children, who never chose to be that way, bear the brunt. They tend to live short lives, their bodies shoved into alleys. Most of the time nobody even notices they're gone, thrown out like trash."

Dewey nodded and rubbed the back of his neck. "Doc, you spend a lot of time in whorehouses and Pansy Clubs when you're in the big city, do you?"

"A bit." Doc smiled. "Dewey, I avail you of certain secrets I wouldn't tell other men, given the closeness of our friendship. I'm a curious soul, an explorer of sorts. In my profession, you need to be open-minded about people's proclivities."

"Yeah, you and me both," Dewey said. "I catch them doing things they shouldn't be doing, and you patch them up afterward."

"And speaking of doing things…what do you plan to do about Canner Schultz?"

The very question Dewey had been considering all day.

THE NEXT MORNING, DEWEY saddled up Belle for the first time in several weeks, the horse frisky, high-stepping at having a job to do. The Model T wouldn't make it where he planned to go, the road up Beartooth Pass a jagged trail six feet too narrow for a car. He had a plot map that clearly showed Canner Schultz's claim, which he calculated to be a two-hour ride.

Forty minutes into the trip, Dewy vacillated between cursing Canner Shultz to hell, and pledging to order those Sears pillows. By the time he reached Canner's stake, the pounding pain in his neck was blurring his vision. He tied Belle to a tree a hundred yards from the smoke funneling near the house, checked to make sure his 12-gauge was loaded to capacity then worked his way through the thicket toward Canner's cabin.

"Canner. Canner Schultz. You here?" Dewey yelled as he reached the clearing. There was a tiny cabin, garbage strewn all around, two wooden chairs facing a fire pit in front of the structure, a small corral with Canner's horse maybe a hundred feet off. Dewey blanched when he saw the iron rods propped near the fire pit, wondering if they'd been used on Jacob.

Canner came around the side of the cabin wiping his hands on a dirty rag. "Sheriff. Sure didn't expect to see you all the way up here. What is it you want?"

"Well, I'd start with hello and the offer of some coffee, if you're feeling hospitable. It's a long ride." Dewey motioned at the pot sitting on a grate above the fire.

"Before I welcome travelers, I like to know they mean me no harm. You carrying that shotgun makes me wonder. You here to arrest me?" Canner balled the rag, threw it down, and widened his stance.

"No, I'm here to talk, and hopefully straighten things out. We both know how you can get rambunctious, and you're a big bastard, so I brought this along to make sure things don't get out of hand. If you pledge to control yourself I'd be happy to set it down, as it's damn heavy and I'm tired."

Canner peered at Dewey, then motioned at one of the chairs. "I'll get you a cup. But I warn you, not everyone takes to my coffee. Tends to be a bit thick."

"I'm sure it'll be fine," Dewey said, and set the shotgun down as he took a seat, then reached back to rub his neck.

The coffee was the consistency of the sludge Dewey drained from his Model T's crankcase, but somehow comforting. The two made small talk about mining and the canyon, then Dewey got to the point. "I'm not in the business of breaking up families, but I also can't stand still and see the boy brutalized."

"Sheriff, a man knows his own blood, knows their soul. I'm trying to save Jacob. That's my responsibility. Satan is dirty business, and it's my duty as his father and as a Christian. You got to trust that I know what I'm doing."

"Well, Canner, I don't have any children that I know of, so I'm not one for parenting advice. But I want you to take it easy. You damn near killed him, and he don't deserve that." Canner dropped his head and didn't say a word. "Can you keep in control if I allow him to come back?"

Canner nodded. "Sheriff, I'll do what's best for the boy. You have my word on that."

"The law doesn't allow me to split up a family, and it's against my better judgment that I'm going to trust you on this. Remember, I'll be keeping an eye on you. Saddle-up and I'll take you to him, long as you pledge to treat him better."

Canner looked up, surprised. "He's in town?"

"Nope. I sent him to stay with the Hughes family yesterday, over near Greenough Lake, less than an hour from here. They've got a passel of kids, said one more wouldn't make much difference as long as it wasn't permanent. You know Joseph Hughes?" Canner shook his head no. "No matter, I'll lead you to where they live and let them know it's okay for Jacob to return with you."

Canner and Dewey spent the next hour riding in silence. As they neared the lake, Dewey stopped to let Canner pass. "I have to stretch my knee and take a piss." When he remounted, he followed ten feet behind. Five minutes later, he recognized the tangle of trees where he'd been thrown.

"They live right on the water?" Canner said, and turned with a confused look. "I've fished here, and never noticed a house."

"No, their place is just over the bluff. A new homestead, nice piece of ground." Dewey quietly unholstered his Colt when Canner faced front again. "Canner, something I'm curious about, you being religious and all. Just how does God feel about you buggering your own son?" Canner jerked his horse to a halt, and reared around to face Dewey's raised gun. "Don't go doing anything crazy now. Big fellow like you makes an easy target."

"What in the hell are you talking about? And pointing a gun at me?"

"I'm just trying understand a man that rapes, tortures, and damn near kills his own boy. Learn what makes a sick son-of-a-bitch like you tick."

"Where's Jacob?" Canner demanded.

Belle skittered, and out of his right eye Dewey saw bushes rustling fifty feet away. "Canner, I've unfortunately spent a lifetime thinking about men like you. Men so sick in the head they rape children without the least remorse. Hell, I had a father that was that kind of man, so I don't hold much tolerance for your type."

Canner grew whiter. "Listen, Sheriff, I..."

Dewey interrupted. "Like your boy, I got the hell away from home before my pa could kill me. Left at fourteen and put as much distance between us as I could. Found the army, and that saved me. But I dreamt about him. Still do. And you know what haunts me the most?"

Canner, panicked, shaking his head.

"That I didn't just kill the bastard. Put an end to his foolishness. Even as a kid I could have stabbed him in the heart while he slept, or caved his head in with a rock. The asshole was usually so drunk he would have never heard me coming. But a father has a particular power over a son, so I ran instead."

"You didn't bring me here to get Jacob, did you?" Canner looked both terrified and resigned.

"No," Dewey said as he fired into Canner's chest. The blast knocked Canner backward, horse rearing, his right foot catching in the stirrup as he fell, body dragging as the animal raised-up. Dewey grabbed the reins and settled the horse, then dismounted to free Canner's foot, the air tart with gunpowder and blood. Canner's body spasmed, the fist-sized hole below his throat bubbling dark red. Dewey stared at him curiously, with none of the revulsion he'd felt when he shot the Andrews brothers.

Both horses whinnied as a low-pitched vibration rumbled from the trees. Dewey mounted Belle and grabbed the reins on Canner's horse, heading back up the trail. Midway, he turned as the grizzly roared. The bear barged out of the brush, clamped onto one of Canner's legs, and dragged him into the trees, leaving a bloody trail.

Back in Red Lodge, he rode straight to Doc's house, tying both horses to a post at the back. "That god damn automobile of yours broke again?" Doc said, motioning at the horses.

"Not exactly. I had some official business that couldn't be navigated in my fine Ford."

"And it took two horses?"

"Well, the one here is for Jacob. Figured he might need it. How's the boy today?"

"He's fine," Doc said, looking curious. "I got him doing a little cleaning at the hospital to help pay his board. He's a good worker. He's feeling better, got his strength back. How'd you come across another horse?"

"Belongs to Canner," Dewey said. "I rode up to have a chat with him, but he was nowhere to be found. Didn't want to leave the animal on the off-chance he wasn't coming back. Too fine an animal to starve to death, and I figured I'd give it to Jacob to take care of, at least until Canner shows up. If he does shows up."

"If he shows up," Doc repeated slowly. "You think something might've happened to Canner?"

"You never know. Lot of grizzly action in those parts. A dangerous proposition to be up there all by yourself. Anyway, I have to check in at the office, make sure there hasn't been a crime wave hit Red Lodge since this morning. Maybe we can catch up later for a beer?"

"Sure," Doc said as his friend walked away. "Dewey, you OK?"

Dewey squeezed the back of his neck, then realized with a smile the pain was almost gone. "Yeah, Doc, I actually feel the best I have in a long time." And right then the thought occurred to him that he might not need those new pillows after all.

MIDNIGHT ELVIS

DURING THE DAY, MY father had the appetite of an elderly woman. A single poached egg and a bit of dry toast for breakfast. Lunch, a sliced tomato with a dollop of tuna fish. Later, a monk's dinner, boiled chicken and stringy broccoli spears. Pop's diet belied his physique. He was rhino-shaped, five-foot-eight, sporting Buddha's belly, and weighing-in at least an eighth of a ton.

The explanation? In the wee hours, house deep in slumber, my Dad ate like Elvis. When I was fifteen, I discovered his nocturnal feasts by accident, while sneaking back to my room at 2:00 a.m. after sharing a joint in the park with Dennis Sticka. There was light leaking out the cracks below the door of his workshop, a block garage that doubled as the headquarters for his plumbing business. It sat at the shady edge of the alley, hidden from the house by the wide canopies of three apple trees.

I feared thieves were ransacking his Snap-On tool box. But when I peered through a corner of the single window, I saw my Dad transformed. Clad in tight white slacks and a shirt with billowy bell sleeves, he was hopping around like some kind of Riverdancer, his ancient Lloyds 8-track tape player blaring "Hound Dog". Pirouetting and shaking his big rump, he simultaneously stuffed a loaf of French bread with peanut butter and banana.

For the next hour, I watched him gyrate with moves I never thought possible for a guy of his dimensions, flailing an air guitar, his lips curled in that famous Presley sneer. In-between dance steps performed to Elvis' greatest hits, he would chow down as if it were his last meal: bowls of Rocky Road ice cream slathered with whipped cream, Snickers bars, green olives plunked from a gargantuan tub, then stuffed into his face while he did the twist.

When I looked out the window the following week, the lights were on again, and I snuck to the shop. Dad was dressed in his Sunday gray suit and what appeared to be tap shoes; his workbench covered by a half-eaten pizza, an empty chicken bucket, and a decimated Sarah Lee cheesecake. Apparently, he was feeling elegant, sipping cheap Chianti, and tap dancing on stained concrete to Dean Martin's "Volaire." His back to the window, he was hoofing-it in front of the Able Plumbing Supply calendar, as if dancing with a scantily-clad Miss February.

Seven days later, Pop was in a soulful mood, rotating between The Temptations, Marvin Gay, and The Isley Brothers. Decked out in the used tuxedo he'd bought at Goodwill three years earlier when he became an officer in the Knights of Columbus, he was styling it casual, collar unbuttoned, sans tie, as he swayed to "My Girl," and "I Heard It Through the Grapevine." His Crescent wrench transformed into a microphone, he bowed up and down, then shimmied sideways like a Pip as he mouthed the words. In-between songs he would snack from a big tray of salami and cheese that sat on top of his tool box, or grab a fistful of peanuts from the half-gallon drum next to the stereo, washing it all down with a Great Falls Select beer.

And so it went, my father sneaking to the garage once a week for a dinner and dancing with himself. His musical tastes were surprisingly varied, running the gamut from The Rolling Stones, to Tom Jones, to Italian opera, his culinary preferences tending toward delicious but very unhealthy.

And I remained a silent observer. Sometimes I considered confronting him, anxious to share a dad and lad secret with the assurance I'd never tell a soul. One night, as he read me the riot act after I was caught stoned and stinking of Coors, I almost let it slip.

"If you can go off to the shop to drink and dance I should be able to have a little fun too," I almost protested, but luckily contained myself.

I knew the pure joy Dad received from his late night parties, and I couldn't risk robbing him of the hour or two he dedicated all to himself. My father spent his days unclogging toilets, pulling grimy hairballs out of drains, and dodging rats and spiders while shimmying under houses. When he wasn't working, he was mostly giving.

He gave the two smallest fingers on his left hand to the Vietnamese at the Tet Offensive. He gave his wife the little house near Pioneer Park she'd always wanted. He gave his demented old mother unlimited love and a sunny little room in our home. He gave every spare dime to his kids' college funds so we could have an experience he could never afford. He gave his evenings and weekends to his family, squiring us to band concerts, basketball games, and Mom's Zonta Club and church fundraisers.

So I figured, if once a week he wanted to party like Elvis, who was I to interfere?

Of course, my mother, continually frowning at his expanding waistline, would express her concern. "I just don't understand it," she'd shake her head. "You eat like a bird, but you just get bigger and bigger."

"Guess I just have a slow metabolism," he'd smile, while patting his rock star belly.

COSTCO GIRL

My foray into manhood occurred on my sixteenth birthday. An unexpected present, conceived under the influence of Billy Beer, or what we called piss in a can, and consummated on the hard vinyl backseat of my mother's 1974 Datsun.

The girl I lost my virginity to, I no longer remember her name, though I swear I knew it then. K rings a bell. Kim or Kris? Katrina? In my own defense, she was older, a senior, and from a different school. I was at the time sexually inexperienced, free from the loutish behavior that ultimately becomes some men's calling card.

It still confounds that any female back then envisioned me sexually worthy. I was a bundle of insecurities, with all the eroticism of an adolescent Barney Fife. My body, rail-thin. I shuffled head-down, angry acne mapping my face, voice in constant hormonal imbalance. We're talking hoarse to falsetto, like a British police siren. My wardrobe consisted of frayed Hash big-bell jeans that hung midway down my flat ass, topped by quilted shirts embroidered with starbursts or eagles, in homage to The Grateful Dead. Plus, a hammered peace-sign on a silver chain.

To make matters worse, I suffered a slight limp. Nothing too serious, just a minor "hitch in the giddle" as my mother sometimes joked, but noticeable enough to have earned me the designation of Gimpy among a not insignificant number of cruel classmates. "A genetic birth defect," Mom explained, necessitating I wear heavy custom shoes, one heel bigger than the other—Lurch boots. "No big deal," she said. "Your Grandfather had it, and he did just fine, even served in the Army." But that did little to assuage the embarrassment whenever someone yelled, "Hey, Hop Along, hobble over there and get me a beer."

When I met K, I was dumbfounded by the attention, praying for a tongued kiss, and in my wet dreams, a headfirst slide into second base. But K was more ambitious, our moves in the tiny car more Cirque Soleil-like than sexual. Peeling off her skin-tight hip huggers I flew into a window as denim cleared a firm cheek. Her mouth tasted of cigarettes, chocolate, and fermenting Billy. The Charlie perfume she wore burned into my brain.

After my lame performance, I offered a redo, suggesting I could borrow my dad's Bonneville, its wide tufted velour backseat like an automotive upgrade from the Motel 6 to the Ritz Carleton. She didn't bite, expressing no interest whatsoever in seeing me again.

Thirty years flew by, and the evening transformed into a salacious story told and retold over wine or martinis. And then one Christmas, after a long absence I returned to my hometown to visit my family. For the past decade, the pattern had been to spend holidays with my wife's folks in Boston, but since the divorce I was left to return alone to old yuletide haunts, my parents and siblings helping me transition back to the single life. And because they commune best under the influence, adorned with cocktail party finger foods, I headed to Costco.

Before shopping the booze and fake food section, I did the full tour, filling my cart with all the essentials: an eight-pack of Lumitron mini LED flashlights, twenty-four pairs of Champion athletic socks (in case I decided to work out), 250 Keurig coffee capsules (which was weird, given I don't own a Keurig coffee maker, but I suspected one might be waiting under the Christmas tree, and I like to be prepared), a four-by-four foot bag of Bounty paper towels, a pen-sized vacuum called "The Dust Muncher," a Scandinavian-looking device that makes sparkling water out of almost anything. Plus, a weird contraption called "The Perfect Pushup" I'd seen advertised on an infomercial. Against the odds of time and physics, I'd never abandoned the fantasy of thick guns and a defined chest.

Since I hadn't eaten, I was grazing at the tasting stands: mini-duck sausages slathered in a tangy mustard concoction; Captain Wilson's line-caught fish sticks served by a wilted old man in a pirate's hat; mysterious beeflets drowned in barbecue sauce manufactured in a barn by a guy named Spicy Willie. And all washed down with a Chardonnay called "Skinny Wine," obviously designed for the anorexic alcoholic demographic, served in thimble-sized plastic cups. I downed three.

Then to the mixer aisle, where I grabbed gallon jugs of Bloody Mary and Margarita mix. It was there that I saw her, stacking jars of cocktail onions. Even after all that time, I recognized her immediately, Kris, or Kathleen, whatever the K girl's name. I stood back to quietly observe.

Aging, I've learned, is all about expansion and contraction, specifically waist and hairlines, noses and man boobs. And my vision? Well, let me put it this way: The thick black hipster glasses I wore resembled Paul Anka in late-stage career. I still walk with a slight limp, as if I might be a war vet, or an athlete gone to seed.

She, however, was still slim-bodied, hair streaked gray but thick and shiny, her face remarkably fresh. To get her attention I reached down to grab a jar of cocktail onions. "Wow, that's a lot of onions," I said, and when she turned, I saw her name tag. Julie. Right, not a K, but close enough in the alphabet.

"Yep, a hundred martinis worth," she said, and absent any hint of recognition, she handed me the jar and turned back to the shelf.

I wondered, was it embarrassing to be in your late forties and make your living stacking drink garnishes? Perhaps she didn't want to be recognized, though I couldn't help but envision a possible *Pretty Woman* moment. I was no Richard Gere, and working at Costco was light years from being a prostitute. But I was a moderately successful real estate attorney, the kind of man a jar-stacker probably didn't get to date all that often.

"Julie," I said. "Is it you? Remember me?" She turned and peered.

"Mmm, familiar face, but no, I'm sorry, I can't place you." Those same adorable lips half-smiled.

"Don. I'm Don. From high school. You and I went out one night. To the lake." Lake is perhaps an overstatement. It was more a watery gravel pit with a refrigerator semi-submerged in the center. "My mom's Datsun?"

"Yes, wow, Don." She inspected me up and down. "I remember, but your memory needs work. I'm Kate, not Julie." She cocked her head at her name tag. "I had to go in the freezer, so I borrowed Julie's coat."

"Kate," I yelled, clapping my hands a little too enthusiastically. "I knew that. I was thrown off by the name tag. Thought maybe you'd changed your name."

"Changed my name? Like I'm in a witness protection program but hanging out at my hometown Costco," she laughed.

"No, it was silly. Sorry. Kate, it's good to see you. You look great. How are you?"

"Good." She got up from her knees and wiped her hands down the sides of her jeans. Not hip huggers, but they fit great, and I was amazed at how well she was put together. "It's been a long time. In fact, wasn't the last time I saw you your birthday?"

Was she flirting? Searching? And what now? A handshake? A hug?

"Great memory. My sixteenth. I've had a few since then," I said, then uncomfortably waved at the aisle, "Costco. How long have you worked here?"

Kate smiled. "I don't work here. I'm just making a delivery. That's my company," she said, and motioned at the label on the jar: Kate's Cocktail Party, adorned with a flattering line drawing of her face.

"Wow. You've done okay for yourself."

"Onions, olives, maraschino cherries, pickled asparagus, beans…
if it goes in a fancy drink, we make it." She pointed at a section of
shelves, her face everywhere, then at my cart and frowned. "So, Don,
it appears you've grown up to become a caffeine addict that has to
wear white socks. Plus, you're messy?"

I had no memory of the teenage Kate being so witty. I shrugged,
and said, "Kate, any chance you can take a break. Maybe a cup of
coffee? As you can see, I can't go long without it. Really, I'd love to
catch up."

She nodded skeptically. "Tell you what. Let me finish up here,
and I'll meet you in twenty minutes in the cafeteria at the front of
the store. Just follow the smell of bratwurst and burnt pizza. You can
even get a cappuccino there, though I doubt it will measure up to
your high Keurig standards."

I was rolling my cart away when she yelled, "Hey, Don, don't eat
more than two onions per day. They're cured in formaldehyde and
might make you blind." I was really getting to like this woman.

I hurried through the liquor section, filling the cart with booze,
chips, and fat shlongs of salami. Costco, land of the giants, everything
magnified several times its normal size, including the bill, which
came to just under twelve hundred dollars.

Kate was sitting at a lemon-yellow plastic picnic table, furniture
that belonged in a preschool, sipping from a tub of soft drink. The
walls were covered with garish oblong posters advertising Costco-
huge food: twenty-four ounce Cokes, two-handed hot dogs, plate-
sized Kirkland burgers with orange cheese sliming the perimeter
of the plate. Mostly large folks chomped greasy pizza, mega-carts,
and even larger flatbed rollers circling the area like wagon trains.
She had ditched Julie's coat, and was wearing a light blue denim shirt
with the "Kate's Cocktail Party" logo. We spent the first few minutes
immersed in normal catch-up: my escape from home, college, law
school, marriage, and divorce; she staying home, transforming a
gardening hobby into a business after her marriage went bad, two

kids, one grown and one attending our old high school. Classmate talk, the successful and the dead. Finally, the conversation turned to our special night.

"So I guess I always just wanted to thank you." I probed the subject carefully. "We never really talked about it afterward. In fact, I barely ever saw you, and I didn't want you to think..." I wasn't sure how to end the sentence.

"Wow, all those years ago and still feeling man guilt over our little romp?" She smiled, then leaned in. "No need for that. Truth is, I was the one that felt guilty. You know, with the herpes thing and all."

I was relatively sure I'd never suffered from a communicable disease, other than the one case of venereal warts in college. I flushed. Was she joking? "The herpes thing?"

Kate laughed. "I'm kidding. Back then I was as pure and clean as they come."

My face heated with relief and embarrassment. "Kate, I always wanted to ask, why me? I mean... You were...you are, gorgeous. You could've had your choice of anyone."

Kate, on the verge of a laugh, said, "Maybe I had a different attitude than other girls. You were cute and funny. Sometimes shy equals sexy."

Sexy. Not a word normally associated with me. Shy. Which could actually mean average.

"Thanks, but I was pretty stunned."

"So stunned that you couldn't remember my name?"

"I know. I'm sorry. Maybe shocked is a better description. I couldn't believe it happened. And then you were gone. As in end of story."

"A lifetime ago," she said. "But it's great to see you. I'm happy things turned out well, and that you're healthy and successful enough to take expensive shopping trips to Costco."

"So, why didn't you want to see me again?"

"God, Don, has that bothered you all these years?" She reached across the table and squeezed my hands. "It had nothing to do with you. I was older, in a different school. The situation wasn't right for us. But c'mon, it was fun."

I nodded with a sense of relief, then was struck by an idea. Perhaps there was a higher purpose to my Costco trip, as mad as it may sound. "Listen, my family is having a little cocktail party tomorrow night. Well, okay, maybe not so little," I said, and gestured at the cart. "There will be a lot of cocktail onions, and I think you'll enjoy the duck sausage. You can meet my little brother, Phil, who I suspect is a transvestite, though he tends to keep his fashion choices private. How about joining us, and maybe afterward we could have dinner?"

She pulled back her hands. "Normally, I'd love to, but I'm booked, and the other thing? I'm seeing someone I'm pretty serious about. I doubt he'd understand me going out with an old high school flame."

Right, so much for my fantasy. "Sure, I understand. I'd feel the same way," I said with undisguised disappointment.

A young man wearing a shirt identical to Kate's sidled up to the table. "Mom, sorry to interrupt, but we're going to miss our delivery slot at Whole Foods."

Kate looked from her watch to me. "Don, this is my son, Terry. The brains and brawn of our little cocktail empire. Terry, Don is an old high school friend of mine who I haven't seen in forever." Terry shook my hand. He appeared to be in his late twenties or even early thirties, too old to be her son. She'd apparently started early.

"Nice to meet you, and sorry to break up the reunion."

"Yep, duty calls," Kate said, rising. I stood and she moved forward with a hug and kiss on the cheek. "Don, so great to see you."

"You too. And, hey, if things ever change…"

She patted Terry on the shoulder and said, "Back to work".

I watched them walk away, and as they reached the sliding doors at the front of the store, I noticed Terry walking with an almost imperceptible limp, the heel of his right shoe appearing just a touch taller than the left, his own little "hitch in the giddle."

EVERYONE LOVES MEAT LOAF

PEGGY GAVE HER BIG brother that look, the skeptic face normally reserved for her four-year-old son when he announced he could fly, or had mysteriously become a black belt in karate. "You quit your job to start a band?" She grimaced at the mediocre Chardonnay the waitress had just set down. "What's the punch line to this joke?"

"No punch line. No joke. I just wanted you to know what was going on. Big changes in my life. We'll rehearse a few weeks, then hit the road. We'll be touring a lot. I probably won't see you as much," Frank announced.

"Okay, my biggest fear is that you aren't kidding," Peggy said, tapping her index finger on the table to contain her anger. "Frank, I know you've been in the midst of some kind of freaky mid-life crisis since Cindy left you. I kept my mouth shut when you got the awful haircut and ridiculous tattoos. I didn't say anything when you started wearing those gross leather pants, and traded your beautiful Mercedes in for that creepy old hearse..."

"It's not a hearse, it's a 1962 Lincoln with suicide doors," Frank interrupted. "A classic."

"Whatever," she snapped. "Whatever the fuck it is, it isn't normal. You are fifty-two-years-old. Middle aged. Not at a time in your life when leather pants and a nose ring are flattering. For God's sake, have a little dignity. Have you forgotten you're a highly paid, respected lawyer? An important guy in this community? You can't start looking like a homeless gay sailor, hanging around dive bars with twenty-year-old crack heads, and then announce you're starting a band. You don't even play an instrument."

"Not true," Frank smiled calmly. "I play the iPad guitar. Been playing almost six months, and I'm pretty damn good. There's an app for that," he laughed. "And I sing. Been taking lessons. Trust me Sis, this is a good thing. We'll be really big."

Peggy pushed fingers hard into her temples. "And what kind of music does your band play?"

"Meat Loaf," Frank said, as if announcing the winner of the Nobel Prize.

"Meat Loaf? The crappy food, or the pudgy guy from the seventies?" Peggy couldn't believe this situation could get even stranger.

"Meat Loaf—Mr. Marvin Lee Aday—one of the greatest rockers of our time. C'mon... "Paradise by the Dashboard Light," "Bat Out of Hell," "I'd Do Anything for Love." He's sold over eighty million albums. Still sells a couple hundred thousand a year," Frank said defensively. "People absolutely love him. He's timeless. And they're going to love our take on him."

"So you're going to abandon a thirty-year career and all the money. What do you make, three, four hundred grand a year, to be in a cover band for a washed-up act from forty years ago? Maybe play weddings at the Butte, Montana Elks Club?"

Frank smiled serenely at his sister, like a man that had solved life's most difficult problem.

~

ELEVEN MONTHS LATER, HE was sitting in the Green Room at *The Tonight Show* when Jimmy Fallon burst through the door. "Frank, oh my God, I'm so happy you're here. I'm a huge fan. Huge. I saw you last weekend at the Hollywood Bowl, playing with the symphony. Un-fucking-believable. I've never seen anyone wail on an iPad the way you do. And stretching "Paradise by the Dashboard Light" into an operetta. That was brilliant."

Frank gave Fallon the same knowing smile he had flashed at his sister. "Thanks Jimmy. Everyone loves Meat Loaf."

BOUNCING

I WAS WORKING THE rope at Tao when Assholio broke through the line. I love the place, but Vegas is ground central for dicks. A town constructed on cleavage and free booze, where morons decked out in Ed Hardy pay five hundred bucks to see circus acts performed to old Beatles tunes. You want to see idiots in hyper drive? Spend an evening doing my job, corralling drunks into any of the hot clubs. Everyone's a big shot in Vegas, a plumber from Oxnard suddenly channeling Tony Montana.

At least a dozen times a night, some dude tries to impress his girlfriend by laying down a line of bullshit to get past me. "I'm a friend of Donny's," they say, as if I know who the fuck Donny is. Or, "Hey, I'm on the high-roller list, just talk to my casino host." When that doesn't work, they flash a twenty, like I'm going to disrupt the fragile dance club ecosystem for twenty dollars. They don't understand that a genuine master of the universe never has to demean himself that way. A real high roller discretely passes me a rolled-up Benjamin or two in a hand shake, like we're old war buddies, then confidently strolls to his table to pound back a fifteen-hundred-dollar bottle of Cristal.

But the jerk pushing his way through the line was not that guy. He looked to have a little Hajji in him, greasy hair and decked out in something from the Men's Warehouse sale rack. Now, I don't want to sound prejudiced against our Arab brothers, even though I wasted two years of my life dodging their IUD's in Iraq. When I say Hajji, that's just my code for any swarthy type. Iranians, Greeks, hell, even

Italians tend to get on my nerves; pushy and talking fast without saying anything. My guess was that Assholio was from the Valley, the mixed-race descendant of a hardworking, olive-oil eating immigrant who owns a dry cleaner or convenience store, and the ditzy blonde he knocked up. Junior was probably taking a break from his job working for daddy to blow off steam with his goombah brethren.

That being said, you had to admire his moxie. He was right in my face, all five and a half feet of him, crowding my six-foot-four frame, spouting some nonsense about his friends being in the club. "See, they sent me a text. They're waiting for us inside," he says as he points at his phone, like that makes any difference to me. The buddies standing next to him are of the same lineage; zit-faced nerds dressed in Lakers jackets or suits a size too large.

I'm a trained professional, which meant I couldn't tell these boys the sad truth; that there was no chance in hell they were getting into Tao on a weekend. Hey, I know it's not fair, but we only populate our dance floor with pretty girls, size six or smaller, and guys that are either handsome or rich enough to take them home. If it were up to me, I'd be happy to admit a few average Americans into the hallowed halls of Tao, but management is strict about their brand.

Unfortunately, these dudes belonged downtown at a low-rent strip club, where hookers flirting with retirement might throw them a little love. "Sorry pal," I say holding up a hand, "back of the line, but my advice, you should find another club, because we're booked-up for at least the next couple hours. Don't want to see you waste your night standing around."

But this guy, probably drunk or flying on some kind of party powder, gets on me. "Listen, I told you my group is already in there, spending a shit load of money, and they're waiting for us," he yells with too much attitude. Then he actually tries to shove past me.

Stupid move. I'm not a guy that gets shoved. Ever. I clock-in at two twenty, and I guarantee you'd need to pinch hard to find even a hint of fat. I've flattened coked-up NFL linebackers when they got rambunctious, so this guy was not a problem. I grabbed him by his six-dollar tie, his arms wind milling, and escorted him outside the rope. "You're gone," I say, "and don't come back."

And believe it or not, Assholio freaks and takes a swing. I intercept his skinny arm, stretch it around his back, and drop him calf-roper style to the floor, placing a knee dead center on his spine. I'm not pissed; it's part of the job, and since I know at least a dozen people are filming us for their "what happens in Vegas video," I'm as gentle as possible, but he goes nuts, hollering like I was vice-gripping his cajones. Once he's on the deck and under control, I tap my ear bud to request security, and within sixty seconds backup arrives, two guys in red blazers to escort him and his friends outside.

"I'm going to fuck you up," he spits at me as they lead him away. "You won't even see it coming. You're dead. You're fucking dead." He's wearing a pit-bull face, and even though he's a plebe, it's a little disturbing.

"Yeah, right," I say. "You boys have a real good night, and I better not see you in here again." And then I forget about it, and I'm back to surveying a giggling group of pretties to decide who gets the golden ticket.

Twenty minutes later, I get a text: Care to help babysit a couple whales tonight after your shift? It's from Lizzy, the head of hotel security. Lizzy's the reason I'm here, Semper Fi and all that, and the truth is I owe her my life. We did our basic together at Parris Island, and became friends over a few hundred beers. Nothing hinky, though Lizzy's a looker if you're into big Swedes with walnut-cracking thighs, but we've never gone there. We had similar backgrounds that drew us to the Corps, and spent many nights commiserating our miserable childhoods. I shipped off to Iraq, and since the Marines don't put women in combat—even though Lizzy is one of the scariest motherfuckers I've ever met—we didn't see each other for almost four years.

I was a mess after my tours, close to becoming one of those guys you see mumbling to imaginary friends while living out of a shopping cart. Lizzy had risen in the ranks through intelligence in the Corps, and afterward got a big job running security at The Venetian. "Come to Vegas," she said, "I'll give you a job, sort out your shit, and you can bang cocktail bunnies." It was supposed to be temporary, but three years later I'm still here.

I substituted weight lifting and martial arts for the booze and drugs that had soothed my disturbed personality. I read self-help books and eat a lot of kale. I'm eighteen credits toward a business degree at UNLV. One day a week, I go to the VA to help some of my equally screwed-up brothers try to assimilate. I still have nightmares, but they're tolerable, and for the first time I have big plans for my life. But right now I'm happy bouncing the lounges, and occasionally providing security for some of the high rollers that come to the hotel.

In fact, if I'm seducing some beauty, my stated profession is bodyguard, as the ladies find it more alluring than being a bouncer. But the job isn't as exciting as Kevin Costner would have you believe. Mainly, I'm clearing a path through crowded clubs and restaurants for rich dudes who get a kick out of having security, sometimes getting them cocktails or bringing girls to the table. But the extra pay is fantastic—it keeps my closet stocked with black Tom Ford suits— and you meet a lot of interesting people.

I buzz Lizzy, and she tells me that she and I will relieve another security detail at midnight. Our client is some dot com billionaire and his girlfriend. He's been playing cards in the big-boy room, is up almost a million dollars, and now wants to party with the commoners, as long as Lizzy and I can make sure the little people don't get too close. I smell an obscene tip.

At 11:00 p.m. I'm done at Tao, which leaves enough time to rush home and change into a fresh shirt, and strap-on a little Ruger LC9 against the low of my back. I've never had to draw a weapon on one of these gigs, but the client wants to know I'm carrying. It completes the fantasy.

Lizzy's waiting for me outside the poker room, looking like a Nordic princess warrior in her sleek silver pantsuit. She reminds me of a Bond girl, especially knowing there's a sexy little chrome Beretta tucked in an ankle holster under those bell bottom pants. The team we're replacing, Patty and Phil, give us the briefing. We run a male / female detail when we're covering a couple, so our woman client is always covered, even in the bathroom. "So far so good," Phil nods at the couple. Phil's craggy old-school Vegas, with a pit boss's demeanor. He's somewhere around sixty, though he's the kind of guy that probably always looked old; a retired cop goosing his pension. "Easy one. He's been playing cards all day, and starting a few hours ago he really began kicking ass. He's some kind of Einstein, counts cards, that kind of thing. Wish I could bet with him. Sarah, his girlfriend, just watches and sips Cosmopolitans. Sometimes she gets up to pee and walks around the shops. Patty says she dropped five large just on lingerie. He drinks Diet Coke with a lime, and just stares at his cards, probably running mathematical calculations like some kind of human IBM computer."

Lizzy and I hover in the corners for the next twenty minutes, and suddenly our guy, Mr. Demorest, signals he's done. I notice he tips the dealers ten thousand each, and the cocktail waitress a grand, which makes me feel all warm and fuzzy inside. I've had my eye on a Ducati Scrambler to take on midnight rides through the desert when the demons refuse to let me sleep, and Demorest might be my patron.

He says he wants to have a drink and wind-down, then hit a dance club. I suggest the Foundation Room at the top of the Mandalay, and we rush Demorest and Sarah through the casino and into a stretch parked outside a private entry.

My man Bobbie G. is covering the door at the Foundation. Bobbie's ex-Ranger with two Afghan tours. We met at the VA a year ago, I made a few calls to get him into the trade, and now we spend some time at the gym together. The man's all pecs. I reach out, and he has a nice table at the back of the room set-up, walls on two sides which makes establishing a perimeter a lot easier.

Demorest seems to be coming out of his card-counting fog; perking-up and turning out to be a friendly guy. He orders a dirty Stoli martini, and we actually have a bit of a conversation. He asks the same questions clients always ask: "What's it like being a bodyguard? Who is the most famous person you've ever guarded? (I always answer Johnny Depp even though it isn't true.) Are you carrying a gun?" I let him pat the little lump on my back, which produces a wide smile.

Demorest tells me he started several app companies. I know most of the names and use one of them to buy movie tickets. Lizzy asks if there's any particular threat we should be aware of. Most of the time clients just say, "No, a guy in my position just needs to be careful," which is code for "I think it's cool to have a bodyguard."

But Demorest gets serious and drops his voice. "There could be an issue." He doesn't want Sarah to hear. "We bought a website based in Russia, and the deal didn't go down very well. I had a pretty tense meeting with the owners yesterday, and they weren't happy. Made a few threats. These guys tend to take things personally. That's why I thought it might be a good idea to have you around until they have a chance to cool off."

I have a hard time believing Russian mobsters would come to Nevada to whack an American billionaire, but it did sharpen me up a bit. When you bounce, the scariest dudes to confront are the Russians, Serbs, and Chechens. Especially the ones built like rhinos, with shaved heads and tattoos covering the back of their hands. They have these dead eyes; like they've spent an afternoon or two stacking bodies. In Iraq, you learn there are two kinds of human beings; the kind that only kill because they absolutely have to, and those that do it because they think it's so much damn fun. I'm always careful when I encounter the latter.

So Lizzy and I scan the crowd more carefully, keeping watch for anyone that looks like he might be pals with Putin. Demorest slams another cocktail, and he's in high spirits and ready to do some clubbing. We end up at Rain at The Palms, parking them on a raised private booth with a great view of the dance floor. I like the fact we're against a wall so Lizzy and I can control access.

Demorest might be a geek, but once he's buzzed the man parties like a Kid Rock, switching from vodka to champagne, amped-up and smiling. He even pulls out a fancy little vape pipe, cupping it in his right hand, toking-up all discrete-like. "Just between you and me," he leans in, "I took your casino for $1.2 mill today."

I give him a surprised grin, even though I already knew the number, and we attempt an awkward high-five. "Great job Mr. Demorest. They can afford it, but I gotta to tell you, it's a rare man that takes their money. You really got some game."

Demorest eats it up. Something I've noticed, no matter how old, rich, and powerful a man becomes, he still seeks the approval of his dad and the high school quarterback, and people always assume I wore the main jersey. I could hear that Ducati purr grow louder.

Demorest and Sarah get up to dance. I anticipated he'd hit the floor like a spastic monkey, but the man actually had a groove. They're blaring this trance crap that does nothing for me—I'm more a rock and roll guy—but the two of them looked great, probably warming up for the lingerie show Sarah had planned for later. Not that I'd know, but I also suspect winning a million dollars is a pretty good aphrodisiac.

A dance floor is a tough place to cover, and Lizzy and I get as close as we can without blowing the fun. All of a sudden, I see three Pravda-types take a table to the left of the floor. Demorest spots them too, and his happy-stoned-fucked-up-face gets pasty, like he's about to heave. We escort them back to the table. "They're here," he says in a shaky voice.

Lizzy and I both know who he's referring to. "Who are they?" she asks.

"The Russians. The guys I told you about. They must've followed me from San Francisco. It's too much of a coincidence that we both just happen in Vegas at this club."

"Alright," Lizzy says. "Let's leave. We'll take the service entrance at the back. I'll have the car waiting. They won't be able to use that exit."

Demorest looks at his drink for a minute, then shakes his head. "No, no…this is bullshit. I did a perfectly legal deal with them. We're not in Moscow, and I'm not going to be intimidated or run out of a club. What are they going to do, beat me up in front of two hundred people? They're just here to scare me, make my life miserable. If I leave, they win, and I'm not going to let that happen."

And suddenly, I really do love this guy, and not just for the monster tip I see on the horizon. You've got to admire a geek that stands up to the Russian mob, even though my job was going to get a lot more difficult.

"Mr. Demorest, are you sure? I'm not comfortable with the security risk," Lizzy says.

"I'm positive." Demorest swigs a glass of Dom. "And now I want to dance." And with that we follow them back out to the floor. Lizzy takes a position ten feet to the right of the Russian's table, and I see her reach into her jacket pocket and ball-up her fist. I know she keeps a sweet little ball-bearing sap in there that leaves a big dent when vigorously applied to a man's forehead, and I think, *God help the Russians if they make a move on our clients.*

The crowd is surging. They've switched from the techno-crap to some kind of Eminem set, and the floor is crowded. I stay within a few feet of Demorest and Sarah, shuffling my feet to blend in, but I know I look silly; one of those big sad lugs dancing by himself.

A group of six or eight partiers in the midst of some kind of ecstasy-groove-love-fest surround me. Two of the girls start rubbing up and down my legs, like cats scratching a pole. The blonde moves behind me, tracing her hands down my shoulders and all the way to my ass. I worry she might encounter the metal lump in my waistband, but her fingers go straight to my gluts. This would be a dream situation if I wasn't working, but I start to slide past them to keep a straight line to the clients.

One of the Russians rises from his table, and Lizzy prepares to intercept him. The truth is, these guys don't concern me. Pudgy and stern—one sporting Breshnev's eyebrows—they don't look particularly tough. If something goes down, I'm confident Lizzy will neutralize them, and I'll cover the clients and hustle them out the back. Plus, Rain's head bouncer, a stocky brother named Teddy, is twenty feet away. He and I make eye contact for a second, and I roll my head toward the Russians so he knows something's up. Teddy's not a man that tolerates bad behavior in his club, and if the shit hits the fan, I know he'll provide backup.

I move a few more steps between the clients and the Russians, but one of the stoned girls pulls at my arm, trying to get me to dance. And then I'm on my knees and falling forward, not clear what's happening. Initially there's no pain, I just lose my ability to move, and I'm on the ground, the girl rushing past me. I reach around the back of my leg, and my hand is coated with oil. No, not oil, I realize; blood, the kind of black blood that pumps out an artery.

I yell, and Demorest and Lizzy turn toward me. Then I'm in total disbelief when I see Assholio, the little jerk from earlier, move out of a crowd of dancers toward Demorest. He's not wearing his shitty suit, so at first I don't recognize him. Now he's dressed in a trim black leather jacket, but I recognize the smirk, as he glances at me and mouths "told you," his right arm swinging wide as he jams something into Demorest's neck before disappearing back into the crowd. Lizzy is rushing toward me and doesn't see it happen.

Demorest is as shocked as I am, reaching to his leaking throat before he falls to the dance floor.

I realize the girl has sliced my femoral artery, probably with a box-cutter or razor, and it dawns on me how truly screwed I am. Lizzy's ripped off her belt to fashion a tourniquet, lynching up my thigh to slow the blood flow, but I know from experience that I've got anywhere from another thirty seconds to a couple minutes to live if the life keeps leaking out of me at this rate. I'd seen it in Iraq; guys with their legs blown off, amazed look on their faces, as they watched their entire blood supply blow out in a pile underneath them.

People are screaming and running as the dance floor floods red. Lizzy doesn't realize what happened to Demorest because her eyes are on me, urging me to relax, purring that everything will be fine in a voice that says it won't. I can see the Russians watching, and I wish I had the energy to reach around and pull my gun so I could blow the smug looks off their faces.

But more than anything, I feel foolish. Lizzy and I were amateurs, allowing them to get at Demorest. We should have known better. I'd forgotten the big lessons I learned overseas; that the ten-year-old kid sidling up to you might shoot your balls off or be wearing a suicide vest. Expect the unexpected, because things are not always as they appear.

Lizzy's shaking me now, and I'm trying to apologize. I know how much flak she'll take for this, but I'm not sure she can hear me.

ADOLPH'S RETURN

ADOLPH BLINKED AWAKE IN confusion. For a moment he assumed he'd gone blind, and then realized he was in pitch black. The air, fetid, almost too thick to breathe, with an odor so foul with decay it made his stomach burn. He wheezed deeply, nostrils coated sticky. He attempted to raise an arm, but was unable to move, his body somehow bound, which explained the deep ache that pulsated in his spine. Shaking his head, he discovered a heavy chain encircling his neck, tethering him to something in the darkness. This was not good.

His last memory was the bunker. Eva had easily succumbed to the cyanide capsule he'd placed between her lips after kissing her goodbye, her complexion now the ivory hue of the dead. Still, Adolph thought she looked beautiful, like a Gabriele Münter painting; her tiny form compressed into the green velvet couch he'd transported to their underground hideaway from The Berghof.

He was more distressed about his beloved dog Blondi and her two pups, their corpses shoved carelessly into a corner in the next room after his aide had tested the suicide pills on the animals a day earlier. It seemed a cruel end for such fine canines, but the last thing Adolph wanted was to be writhing in pain or shitting his pants from too low a dosage when the Russians broke through. He knew what the barbarians would do if he was discovered alive. He remembered popping the capsule, chased with a swallow of rare Chateau de Laubade Armagnac the SS had looted from a French palace, and then placed the Walther into his mouth before pulling the trigger. And then…this.

It occurred to him that he might be buried alive. Perhaps the gun had misfired, and he'd collapsed into a coma from the cyanide, only to awaken six feet under in a pine box.

Or did this indicate something more glorious? Could he be rising from the dead, somehow beating mankind's most inevitable foe? Of course, he'd sometimes pondered his own immortality, given the god-like powers he possessed. He recalled standing on the terrace at the Reich Chancellery, two hundred thousand Germans below, arms raised in salute while chanting his name in adoration. A man that elicited such a response from the masses could have unlimited potential.

His tongue, leathery and swollen, was caked with what tasted like sour milk, but he was unable to spit away the foulness. An hour or two passed, and suddenly the darkness was broken by the sound of a heavy door sliding, a column of light stretching in front of him. He was thrilled to discover he wasn't underground but in a barn surrounded by small cattle stuffed into tiny chutes, their heads chained to posts. He squirmed hard, but because his head was also chained he couldn't lower his gaze to see how we was restrained. What kind of mad jail is this?

"Don't struggle, Mein Führer, it just makes it worse." Adolph traced the voice, but all he could see was the cow facing him across the aisle. The animal's lips were vibrating a faint bray, but somehow he could hear words from the beast.

"Did you speak?" What kind of world possessed talking cows?

"Ah, Mein Führer, you've once again lost your memory, haven't you," the bovine said sadly. "It's me, Himmler."

"Heinrich? Heinrich Himmler? How could this be?" Adolph stared at the nodding animal.

"Yes, Mein Führer. As I have often explained to you, the two of us seem to be on a perpetual journey. This is one of many stops we've made, and I suspect we will make many more."

Adolph gasped. "But you...you're a cow?"

"Yes, this time we are cows. Or to be more precise, veal." Himmler's sad cow-eyes blinked. "Soon, the man that entered the barn will be feeding us a particularly unappetizing milk."

"Veal?" Adolph jerked his head while raising an arm. No, not an arm, a hooved leg.

"I think this is our third or fourth time returning as veal. I can't keep track, and you seem to completely lose memory from life-to-life," the cow said. "This is certainly not one of my favorites, but far preferable to some of the other's we've lived. For me, the worst is reincarnating as a goose, force fed to make foie gras. I detest the stuff."

"I don't understand," Adolph said in panic. "We reincarnate?"

"Yes, and, unfortunately, we rank very low on the karmic scale. We've returned as pack mules, factory chickens, occasionally sewer rats—that's really foul—sometimes foxes or rabbits to be hunted. Often we're small animals trapped in laboratories where they do the most dreadful things to us. And oh, I almost forgot about the insects. It is terrible to wake up as a spider or grub, only to be eaten by a bird. The only compensation is that it's a very short life. Probably best you don't remember."

"Always animals? Never as humans?"

"Once, many lives ago, we were babies somewhere in Africa. But we quickly starved to death, blanketed with flies in a muddy hut. Just dreadful. All in all, the animal lives are preferable."

"Heinrich, I don't understand. You and I…we're extraordinary. Leaders of the master race. How could this happen?"

"Adolph," the cow said in exasperation. "How often must we have this discussion? Every time you wake up it is the same question. Why? Why? I don't know. Who can understand such things? My biggest fear is that our new life might be a thousand year Reich that we are just beginning."

Adolph shook his head. "But, Heinrich, It's…"

He was cut short as a man shoved a bucket of milk into his snoot, strapping the container snugly behind his ears. "Drink up buddy," he said cheerfully, "All you can eat. Get nice and fat, my pretty little twenty-buck-a-pound veal."

HOMELESS GARY BUSEY

IAN DAVIS WAS AN orderly man. His closets: length and style-organized on color-coded hangers with pleasing symmetry. His refrigerator: logically structured by height and food type, anything with pending expiration dates moved weekly to the front. He scrubbed his kitchen within minutes of use, and robotically made his bed every morning—always before showering—with military-tight corners.

His work-day uniform rotated between identical pressed Banana Republic chinos and a blue denim shirt, topped by a cotton sweater or navy blazer on cooler mornings. Weekday breakfasts always consisted of Kashi Vanilla Oats, adorned with four ounces of Greek yogurt and a handful of blackberries, consumed while listening to *Morning Edition.*

Monday through Friday at 7:15 a.m., prompted by his iPhone alarm, he religiously commenced the twenty-minute walk to work. Preparations for the journey included filling his NPR travel mug with French press coffee, then buckling-up the Tumi shoulder bag that housed his laptop, water bottle, and two Granny Smith apples. He kept a tiny copy of *The Twelve Steps* buried in the front flap, but thankfully hadn't needed to pull it out for several months.

Navigating the steep stairs from his apartment onto Cardinal Lane, he traversed the freeway bridge, dropped down into the park that wound through the Portland State University campus, finally arriving at the downtown home of Jazz Technology, twenty-five minutes before he was officially required to be there. Ian found great satisfaction in being prompt.

He was well acquainted with the homeless population that roamed the downtown corridor, and for the last four years since moving to the city, he'd navigated the collision of have and have-nots with few issues. He ascribed to the city's recommendation not to give change to panhandlers, instead donating $100 per year to a shelter he passed on his walk. While most of the street-dwellers were harmless, he learned to avoid the weed-whiffing thugs perched on skateboards congregated across the street from the Art Museum, and stayed clear of anyone openly consuming drugs or alcohol, or engaged in angry conversations with fictional friends.

On a July morning, as he passed a vacant lot bordering the bridge spanning the 405 freeway and the University, an enormous form sprang from chest-high grass, jolting Ian and forcing him to jump off the curb. Wrapped in a tatty wool blanket—Indian-chief style—the massive form was clad in faded gray swimming trunks and a Steely Dan concert T-shirt promoting their 1980 Gaucho tour. His feet, dirt-stained gray, were encased in bright pink flip-flops that looked a size too small.

"Where's my Egg McMuffin?" he screamed.

Sensing potential violence, Ian checked traffic to make sure he could dart across the street. It appeared the man had slept in the field, his blanket mud-caked, strings of hay protruding like knitting needles from his long blonde hair. "Do you have my Egg McMuffin?" He jabbed a filthy finger at Ian.

"I don't know anything about that," Ian tried to respond calmly to avoid exciting him. "I'm just walking by." With that, he rushed across the street, heading toward a group of students congregated in front of a food cart.

"Wait a minute. I want my goddamn Egg McMuffin," the man hollered, giving chase. Ian didn't want to embarrass himself by breaking into full sprint, and instead accelerated to a loping speed-walk into the park. The man, flip-flops smacking, stayed on his heels, yelling, "Give me my Egg McMuffin, you selfish dick. I want breakfast, you faggot dwarf."

Ian breathed a sigh of relief when he spied a group of construction workers near a nearly completed building, and crossed the street in their direction. The man's threats were growing more volatile. "You give me my Egg McMuffin, or I will shit down your pie hole."

"Hey, Gary, calm the fuck down," yelled a burly worker in a hard-hat. "Leave the guy alone."

Ian sidled up to them, and the homeless man stopped ten feet back in the middle of the street. "He owes the toll. One Egg McMuffin."

"I was walking down the street, and the guy started hassling me," Ian countered.

"You crossed my bridge, and I charge a toll. One Egg McMuffin," the man screamed, arms waving in windmill. "I'm the troll of the 405 bridge," he blubbered, then screwed his face into a frightening mask, screaming, "Aghhhh. Give me my breakfast, you pathetic little Nordstrom's yuppie, or you will face my wrath."

"Gary, leave him alone, and get out of here." The construction worker made an exaggerated burst forward, and Gary jumped back, then tried to save face by pantomiming an old-timey boxing stance.

"OK, but tomorrow you will owe two Egg McMuffins, and I will collect, you chiseling mini-man." Gary punched an air jab, then shook a fist at Ian. "I've seen you around. I know where you live, you human skid mark, and I will get my breakfast," he yelled over his shoulder, as they watched him hustle through the trees.

"Thanks a lot," Ian mumbled to the worker.

"No problem. We call him Homeless Gary Busey, 'cause he looks so much like that actor, doesn't he? Maybe it is him. Haven't seen the guy in a movie lately." The man smiled and motioned at the blanketed form halfway across the block. "Don't know his real name, but he's been hanging out a few weeks. Crazy, but I think he's harmless. Just makes a lot of noise."

"Well, I appreciate your help." Ian started down the sidewalk.

"No problem, little fella," one of the other workers yelled with a laugh. "Just come see us if any of those nasty folks in the park bother you."

Ian winced at the "little fella." At five-foot-three, and 125 pounds, he was sensitive about size, and his fear of Homeless Gary Busey was replaced with anger. Anger at being hassled for no reason. Anger at being ridiculed by big, clueless men wearing steel-toed boots. He walked a few feet, stopped, and took a deep breath. *God grant me the serenity to accept the things I cannot change,* he chanted to himself. He needed to keep "Bad Ian" in check, and allowing silly anger to surface could only summon buried demons.

That night, too exhausted to face the prospect of encountering Gary, he decided to Uber home. At times like this he had a strong craving for alcohol, but since he'd been sober for the last four years, he opted instead to splash a little cranberry juice over club soda in a tall glass, pretending it was something stronger. He was sitting on his tiny deck firing up his Hibachi when he heard the commotion.

"I see you," Homeless Gary yelled from the street. "I told you I know where you live. I hope you plan on bringing me my Egg McMuffins tomorrow, or I guarantee, there will be hell to pay. Nobody crosses the 405 troll."

"Get out of here," Ian screamed down. "I'll call the police."

"The police," Homeless Gary said sarcastically. "You think that scares me?" He rolled his arms up, striking a monster pose. "I'm the goddamn 405 troll. The cops have no power over me. This is my kingdom, and you better listen up, you Starbucks-loving anal wart. Tomorrow morning, I want two Egg McMuffins. Nice and hot, too. If I don't get them, I'm going to drag you to my cave, chain you to a wall, and skin you alive. Maybe skull-fuck your tiny head." Gary dropped his hands to his crotch and made an obscene gesture. "You understand me?"

Ian rushed into his apartment and slammed the patio door. He called 911, and a few minutes later met the police car circling the area, but there was no sign of Homeless Gary.

"Not much we can do about it," one of the officers told him. "Some of these guys are pretty whacked out, but they're usually harmless. If he shows up again give us a call."

The next morning, Ian took an Uber to work, deciding it wasn't worth the risk of an encounter. It put him in a foul mood for the day. It's ridiculous I can't use a city street for fear of an insane homeless man, he kept ruminating, which conjured up old angry emotions. On his lunch break he walked four blocks to the police station, and met with a detective to discuss the situation. Once again, the official position was no position.

"A crazy guy yelling a few threats would be impossible to prosecute," the detective told him. "We'd have to put half of Portland in jail. Including the mayor."

"A guy threatens to drag me to a cave, remove my skin, and have sex with my skull," Ian said, "and the police can't do anything about it?"

The detective shrugged and smiled. "Let me know if he actually does any of those things. That would make for a good case."

"Funny guy," Ian said in disgust. "How about getting him help? He's obviously got mental issues. He shouldn't be on the street. He needs treatment."

"He and a few thousand others living out there," the detective said. "There's no budget for those folks. You can look around, but we don't have anywhere to send them."

That night, Ian Ubered home again. Just after 7:00 p.m., he was cleaning his kitchen when he heard a loud thump on the patio door, a jagged crack spiraling-up from the bottom. Assuming a wayward bird had slammed into the glass, he rushed out onto the patio. A stone whizzed above his head. "Where the fuck are my Egg McMuffins?" Homeless Gary was standing fifteen feet below, a bright fuchsia women's bathrobe pulled tight around his shoulders like a cape. He was wearing sweat pants, a tee-shirt promoting the 1983 ZZ Top "Sharp Dressed Man" tour, and a filthy cream fedora, an eagle feather spouting out the top. His flip-flops had been replaced by huge unlaced work boots, and his fists bulged with rocks.

"I warned you, but you just don't listen, you half-pint J-Crew scumbag. Now you will pay the price. And the toll has risen. Tomorrow I want three Egg McMuffins, and two Big Macs. Breakfast and lunch. First thing in the morning. And if I don't get them, I promise I will drag you to the cave, cut off your dick and ears, and feed them to you. Might even spit roast you. I'm not kidding." Ian dove to the deck as more rocks struck the door. When he peeked over the side of the patio Gary had disappeared.

Terrified, Ian slumped back into the apartment, carefully double-locking the patio slider, dropping the shade, then rushing to the front door to make sure it was secure. He combed through his medicine chest until he found the Xanax he'd squirreled away several years earlier—for an emergency. Ignoring the long-past expiration date, he threw two in his mouth and bent down to drink from the faucet.

Returning to the kitchen, he reached into a corner cabinet to retrieve a bottle of Merlot, dubbed "Jazz Wine" on the label, a company Christmas gift he'd hidden after the holiday party—just in case he made a friend. Uncorking the bottle, Ian hesitated for a second to consider his hard-fought years of sobriety, but hands shaking, decided this was a dire situation that required medication— and this was really just medicine, he told himself—pouring a tall glass. Grabbing an aluminum softball bat out of the closet, he sat at the kitchen table for the next hour and consumed the entire bottle, waiting for Homeless Gary's next move.

The next morning, he awoke on his couch to the chirping of his iPhone alarm. Head throbbing, with serious Mojave-mouth, Ian was suddenly racked with guilt as the previous evening came into focus. How could he have thrown away all those years of progress?

Dread washed over him as he recalled many mornings like this; waking up sick, sometimes in a pool of his own spew, attempting to piece together the previous night and assess the damage he'd done. The awful realizations: that his drunken antics had cost him a job, or perhaps another friend or family member. He'd been sure those days were over, his fresh start in Portland a way to exorcise himself of "cruel drunken Ian." But now, Bad Ian was back. He'd somehow lost control. And all because some crazy homeless fuck had chosen him to harass.

For the first time since he'd started working at Jazz, he called in to tell them he'd be late. He showered and dressed slowly, carefully considering his next steps. Bad Ian had to be put back in his box. Homeless Gary Busey needed to be ejected from his life, though it occurred to Ian that he and Gary might not be so different. Four years ago, if Ian hadn't found the courage to change, to leave Minneapolis and reinvent himself in Portland, to live the program and pursue a virtuous life, he might have ended up on the street too. So he certainly needed compassion. But he also couldn't allow Gary to destroy all he'd built. The program had taught him that sometimes people needed to be removed from your life in order to survive.

Feeling better, he considered this might be some kind of sign; an opportunity to redeem himself while developing more strength. He decided he'd make an attempt to help Homeless Gary, while also making it clear he did not want him in his life. Head still pounding, he showered and dressed, and before leaving the apartment pocketed the pepper spray he kept in the bedside table—just in case.

He walked at half-speed, head swiveling as he approached the 405 bridge, in the hope he might see another commuter. He was halfway past the vacant lot when he heard bellowing from underneath the bridge. "I hope you brought my food." Gary was crawling up the incline, one hand grasping at thick weeds to hoist himself. He'd abandoned the woman's robe for his blanket, and the fedora had been replaced with an ancient steel army helmet with a ripped Bob

Marley sticker on the front. He was carrying a toy plastic light sabre. "You know, you look like a man, only smaller," he chortled, then his face grew serious. "Now show me my fucking Egg McMuffins, or face the consequences. I can easily decapitate you with this thing," nodding at the Star Wars sword.

Standing on the edge of the sidewalk, Ian couldn't decide whether to laugh or run. "Listen Gary, or whatever your name is. Let's stop this. I'll get you food. Good stuff, not just McDonalds, and I'll do more. I can help you get a safe place to stay, and find someone to help you. There are a couple clinics downtown. Walk with me. I'll get you something to eat, then we'll find someone you can talk to."

"Are you insane?" Gary puffed large, eyes rolling. "I'm the 405 troll, you ignorant crack head, and I live down there in my palace cave." He motioned underneath the bridge. "The most luxurious home in the world: hot tub and premium cable, a king-sized Serta Perfect Sleeper. A Sonos sound system." He waved his arms. "I would never leave my kingdom, and I'm not going anywhere with you. I bet you just want to lure me out so evil Balthazar can take over. I know he'd give anything to possess my kingdom. Is that it?" Gary plunged forward, poking at Ian with the toy. "Are you one of Balthazar's agents?"

Ian jumped back, but misjudged Gary's speed, and on his second swing the plastic sword caught him squarely in the jaw with a stinging blow. "Goddamn it. Knock it off." But Gary swung the toy with a backhanded flip, striking Ian hard on the opposite cheek and splitting his lip. The drip of blood on his tongue both terrified and enraged Ian. He crouched, protected his head with his left arm, reached into his pocket with his right, and pulled out the pepper spray. He fooled with the latched top, spraying blindly in Gary's direction. Ian raised his head when he heard a pained scream. He'd hit Gary squarely in the face with the spray. The big man was clawing at his eyes.

"Aagh, you fuck! I'll remove your midget head and put it on a stick." Gary stumbled backward. "I'm going to…" And then, with an even more sickening yelp, Homeless Gary backed hard into the bridge railing, catapulting into a reverse flip over the side.

"No," Ian yelled, cringing as Gary disappeared, then at the accompanying thud, followed by the sounds of horns and locked brakes. He rushed to the bridge railing. On the freeway forty feet below a Volkswagen had skidded sideways across two lanes when Gary crash-landed on the hood. Another car clipped the rear quarter panel jutting into their lane, sending the Volkswagen spiraling. Gary's unconscious body flew into oncoming traffic: first pinned to the grill of a Dodge Ram pickup, then thrown ten feet in the air into the windshield of a speeding Audi, which crashed into a Toyota Tercel, as Gary ricocheted between vehicles like a bloody pinball.

"Holy shit." Ian looked to his left at two college students, one who was filming the entire spectacle with his phone. "Dude," the wide-eyed kid blurted. "What did you spray him with?"

Ian waved his arms in panic. "I was protecting myself. He'd been after me, and I…" He looked down at the pepper spray and flung it over the bridge as he collapsed to his knees. "Jesus. He just fell."

"Protect yourself? Dude, the guy had a toy sword. He couldn't have hurt you. We saw it all. I filmed it. You just blew that guy away for no reason."

"I didn't," Ian pleaded. "You don't understand. He'd been threatening me. He said he was going to…" Ian swiveled his head at the wail of sirens. The kid was holding the camera at arm's length, recording Ian as if he were some kind of science experiment. "I didn't mean to hurt him. I was going to help," he protested as he rose, and began sprinting back across the bridge. By the time he crossed, flashing lights were coming from both sides of the freeway.

Ian ran two blocks to his apartment, bolted the door behind him, and rushed into the bathroom to down the remaining Xanax. *This has to be some kind of bad dream*, he told himself. *I must still be* drunk and having nightmares. He sat on the edge of his bed, gulping deep breaths and waiting for the drugs to kick-in, as he listened to more sirens in the distance.

Thirty minutes later, he turned on the television. A reporter was on the bridge near the spot Ian had stood. At least a dozen policemen wandered behind her stringing crime-scene tape, as another man photographed the scene.

"This is the spot where a homeless man was allegedly thrown to his death off this bridge," the intensely-coiffed woman said. "And in fact, this is also the bridge where KGW News has a traffic cam, so we have the entire horrible incident on video. I must warn you, even though we have edited the footage, this is disturbing and not appropriate for young children."

Ian watched as Gary's body flew by the camera mounted on the lip of the bridge, one flailing hand striking the lens. The footage had the grainy sepia hue of a low-budget horror film, and had been slowed-down so you could clearly see Gary flipping in mid-air before slamming onto the car hood and bouncing between lanes.

"According to police, two college students filmed the entire altercation that led to the man's death, and authorities are currently interviewing witnesses and reviewing the video. Back to you Sheila and Ed," the reporter signed off.

"What a horrible, horrible thing," Sheila the news anchor turned to her sidekick.

"Unbelievable," Ed said, shaking his puffy Botox-enhanced head. "Sometimes in this job you see such unbelievable inhumanity. And now, Les McCord reports on KGW's search for the best barista in Portland."

Ian flipped off the television and began to sob.

Twenty minutes later he opened the door to a gaggle of policemen, many with drawn weapons, led by the detective he'd consulted the previous day. "I guess you decided to take care of the homeless guy on your own," he said, pushing Ian back into the room as he flipped him around to handcuff him. "Bad idea. Ian Davis, you're under arrest for murder."

⏤

IAN FLOATED IN A Xanax high for the next few hours as he was transported to the station and led into an interrogation room. He did have the presence of mind to request an attorney, and as he was sipping bad coffee, emerging from his drug haze, a gray-haired man in a decades-old seersucker suit sat down in front of him. "I'm Jeff Merrick, your lawyer," he said holding out an age-spotted hand.

He looked pleasantly familiar. "You look like Matlock," Ian muttered.

"Let's just hope I'm as good as him," he smiled. "You've got a big mess here. You've been charged with second-degree murder. They have video clearly showing you dousing the homeless man with pepper spray, forcing him over the bridge. They found the container with your fingerprints. They have testimony from a detective that you complained of altercations with the deceased. They have testimony from a group of construction workers that witnessed you arguing with him."

Ian, suddenly feeling very sober, interrupted to explain the last few days. His attorney listened thoughtfully as Ian became increasingly distraught. "Listen, I don't doubt a word of what you're saying," Merrick said. "I'm sure you were afraid and it was self-defense. Our problem now is perception. The videos have gone viral. They're all over the place, even the national news. And the victim, the guy you call Homeless Gary Busey. It turns out his name is Brian Parker. Former Marine. Some kind of hero in the first Gulf War. He suffered from PTSD and was in treatment, but then his wife was killed in the World Trade Center. He eventually spiraled out of control. He's been living on the streets for years, just moving around getting crazier and crazier. Given his background, people have a lot of empathy for him, and they want your head. The DA can see in those videos that Gary was swinging at you, but he can't let you off easy. After all, it was a toy sword. Plus, there's too much political pressure. There are protesters outside right now amped-up like some kind of lynch mob. Congratulations, you're the national bogeyman in the homeless debate. Get ready. Things are going to get ugly."

~

IAN LEARNED THAT UGLY was an understatement. For the next few months, he watched his life be degraded, debated, distorted, dissected, ridiculed, and very occasionally, championed. The videos were edited, played, and replayed to make him appear even more the monster. For weeks, until he was knocked off the charts by a man who attacked a school bus with a machete and an assault rifle, he was the most hated man in America, as various homeless organizations, veteran's groups, human rights advocates, liberal politicians—and even Oprah—vilified him. His rare supporters were a sketchy group; noisy right-wingers, white supremacists, Ted Nugent, and a southern senator best known for calling women "baby vessels" and advocating the use of nuclear weapons on almost everyone.

His alcohol and drug abusing past was detailed on television and in *People* magazine. People he didn't remember came forward to detail confrontations with "Bad Ian" and blame him for the various maladies that impacted their lives. Jazz Technology chose to terminate his employment via a voice mail on his cell phone, and even Uber publicly announced his account had been closed. He was evicted from his apartment, and his sister, who'd disowned him seven years earlier after he'd backed over her cat in a Budweiser-haze, sent him a concise email: I'm embarrassed we share the same blood. Rot in hell.

Ian first observed his demise from a cell in the Multnomah County Jail, as he scrambled to raise bail, then watched his final destruction from the shabby confines of a series of cheap motel rooms, most of them located behind truck stops or in crime-infested neighborhoods. It was dangerous to be Ian Davis—death threats were a daily occurrence—and given his dismal financial situation after the enormous legal fees, he could only afford to rotate between budget accommodations where tenants tended to keep low profiles.

Before his trial, which promised to be big national news, Jeff Merrick strongly recommended he take a plea agreement for manslaughter. "But it was self-defense," Ian protested. "An accident."

Jeff assured Ian he understood, but feared public opinion would prevail. "The DA understands too, but he needs his pound of flesh. Take the deal. You'll do eighteen months in a low-security facility. People will forget about all this, and some other poor sap that was at the wrong place at the wrong time will take your place. It will be a cakewalk, and when you get out you can start your life over."

~

IAN WOULDN'T DESCRIBE THE two years he spent in jail as a "cakewalk." Many of his fellow inmates had been homeless at one time or another, and his crime elicited a certain fury from them. Plus, a man his size, with such delicate features, drew the wrong kind of attention in prison.

Eventually, he was filed-away in a wing reserved for those accused of similarly ironic and non-threatening crimes, assigned to be cellmates with a check forger, and a man who'd been incarcerated because he'd flipped-out and attempted to defecate on an airline serving cart.

But it was true that Ian was largely forgotten when he was released. Six years earlier, when he'd first arrived in Portland from Minneapolis, he'd been filled with determination and enthusiasm to build a new life, anxious to leave Bad Ian behind. But now, stepping off a bus, with all the possessions he'd managed to accumulate in his thirty-nine-years hanging around his shoulder in a cheap duffle bag, optimism was a foreign concept.

He'd spent many nights lying in his cell, conversing in his head with Bad Ian, angrily lamenting that his attempt to lead a good life had led to this. I was better off when I was stoned and an asshole, he'd think to himself in disgust. And once again he'd arrived in Portland devoid of family or friends. Bad Ian is the only one that stuck with me.

He'd been assigned to live in a release center for the next few weeks, but after walking the four blocks from the bus station into Chinatown, Ian realized his new home, The Golden Arms, was a former flea-bag motel that had been condemned, repossessed, and rebranded by the state into a bed-bug infested halfway house.

He recalled walking by the place when it was a haven for low-end hookers and meth heads, and it appeared little had changed in the neighborhood. Twitchy drug dealers flanked both corners, and the perimeter of the parking lot across from The Golden Arms was ringed with shopping carts and cardboard houses for the homeless, as two stocky, heavily-inked men of violent ethnicity—one with a vicious-looking dog tethered to his wrist—watched over the area with hooded eyes.

Ian found there were few professional opportunities for people with felony records, even for a man with his coding skills. He soon found himself wrapped in a hairnet, cleaning deep fat chicken fryers in the back of a Chick-Fil-A. For the first week, he attempted to stay focused and concentrate on logical steps to improve his situation. But Bad Ian was increasingly intervening in his psyche, convincing him there was no upside in the straight and narrow.

One night, at Bad Ian's urging, he stopped for a beer after work. Tiny's Tavern served a hopeless clientele; dishing-up cheap liquor to patrons who purchased their cigarettes one at a time and frequently bathed in the bathroom sink. Ian got very drunk that night, snorted some kind of marching powder he bought for ten dollars, and he and Bad Ian decided they'd had enough of hairnets and halfway houses.

After retrieving his few belongings, he never returned to the Golden Arms or the restaurant.

Six months later, he was camped in the doorway of an abandoned building in The Pearl District when he heard someone repeating his name.

"Ian, Ian, is that you? Are you OK? Can you hear me?"

Ian blinked awake, suddenly very aware of a sharp pain around his kidneys. He had a faint recollection of a fight. Two men, yes... two big muscular men, fireplugs, slathered with tattoos, laughing as they beat him, and they had a dog, a pit bull... He recalled being thrown across a wide stone garbage can in the park, face smashed into the concrete aggregate, as one of them rifled his pockets while the other pummeled his ribs, the dog clamping onto his ankle, chewing his leg like a chicken bone. His hand traced to a pocket on his skinny ass, and he realized with despair they'd taken his last few dollars and a baggie of heroin.

He'd worked hard for that little bit of heaven. Five hundred aluminum cans, plucked from filthy trash bins and hauled to the recycling center, all for nothing. He pulled his hand from his backside, suddenly noticing he'd pissed himself. Not unusual, but for a moment he worried it was because of the beating. Maybe they'd broken something important. It's not safe to be wounded on the street. The weak tend to get hunted down like a lame deer tracked by coyotes. His mind went to the next pain point: his ankle. The dog. He thought about rabies, or at the very least not being able to walk, which could be equally deadly.

"Ian, do you remember me?"

Ian looked through liquid eyes at the man leaning over him. Andy Griffith. He loved Andy Griffith. No, wait, not Sheriff Andy. The other one. Matlock. Matlock was standing in front of him in a rumpled suit. Smiling, with the rosy cheeks of an Irish drunk.

"Ian, its Jeff Merrick. Remember me? I was your lawyer."

"Yeah. Hi." Ian felt momentary joy, but then fear washed over him. The last time he'd seen this man, they'd taken him to prison. He didn't want to go back there. Had he done something wrong that he didn't remember? He tried to rise to his feet, but his left ankle, the chicken bone, gave in, and he fell back to the pavement. His shoe was gone, and a bloody ripped sock appeared grafted to his skin. Then he fell back into a peaceful black.

He awoke in the emergency room on a clean white gurney. Matlock…no, that wasn't his real name. Merrick. Merrick was standing next to the doctor. "How are you feeling Ian?" Jeff looked at him with the only friendly face he'd seen in a long while.

"We sewed up your leg. Nasty bite. You might need surgery on that one. Pumped you full of antibiotics. You took a hell of a beating," the doctor said. "There doesn't appear to be any serious damage, but we need to check you out again in a day or two to make sure there's no internal bleeding. The stitches need to come out in about a week. Also, you're malnourished, and you have some skin issues that should be treated. Half your teeth are ready to fall out."

"Ian," Jeff interjected, "we need to get you some help. You look like hell. I'm going to look into finding you a place…"

"I don't need help. I have a place," Ian lied as he rose from the gurney. "But thanks." He stumbled when his feet hit the ground. The doctor grabbed his shoulder.

"No, Ian…you're hurt. You need to stay in bed." Jeff came around the gurney.

"Mr. Merrick, I'm sorry, but unless you're going to foot the bill Mr. Davis needs to be released. We've handled the critical issues, and I don't have authorization to keep him here any longer. I have a cane we can give him. And he does need to come back. But I'm not allowed to overnight him."

"Well, no, we can't just…" Jeff said in panic.

"It's okay, I'm fine. I want to leave." Ian took the cane and hobbled toward the door. He couldn't recall how he knew this Merrick guy, but it had something to do with prison, and he didn't want to go back there. And thanks to whatever painkiller they'd pumped into him, he felt the best he had in weeks. Jeff continued to protest as they moved to the hospital entry, as Ian refused any additional assistance. Finally, he allowed Jeff to drive him to a shelter, gladly accepting the sixty dollars the lawyer gave him when they parted.

Usually in a shelter he got little sleep, concerned with protecting himself and his few possessions. But still reeling from painkillers, he snoozed soundly in his cot. The next morning, he showered for the first time in weeks, then stopped in a basement storeroom full of donated clothing to pick out a new outfit. Digging through the stacks, he was delighted to find a Hootie and the Blowfish concert T-shirt, promoting their 1994 Cracked Rear View tour.

He had a recollection of seeing them in Minneapolis that year, cheering hysterically as he downed beers and snorted coke off the back of his left hand. He also discovered a pair of Jordache jeans in a child's size that fit, albeit a little lose in the seat, and a Portland Beavers baseball jacket. He completed his outfit with a worn pair of screaming yellow Nike's, and a child's stocking cap, emblazoned with a Hello Kitty logo, that nicely topped his small skull.

Ian wandered the downtown corridor, careful to avoid Chinatown where he might encounter his attackers. Around noon, leg aching and side pounding, he was able to buy another baggy of heroin for twenty dollars from a homeless man everyone called Slim Pickens. The two crawled between Slim's shopping cart and a wide maple tree, and sharing a needle, shot-up while watching a busload of grade schoolers file off a bus and into the Oregon Historical Society.

His pain now obliterated, Ian traipsed through the Portland State campus, moving like a new man. Peering at his reflection in a Starbuck's window, he thought he looked spiffy in his new clothes. The cane not only minimized his limp, it made him powerful, like carrying a pirate's sword.

He waved it in mock-menace at students walking near him. "Aye matey, stay clear or I'll have yer head," he yelled in a bad cockney accent. He was unaware the stitches in his leg had loosened, and everyone gave wide berth to the crazy man waving a stick, blood dripping over his shoes.

As the drugs really kicked in, Ian realized he didn't need to walk, he could actually levitate like some kind of human hovercraft. At the edge of campus, he approached the 405 bridge, suddenly feeling the chill of déjà vu. He'd been here before. There was something important about this place. At the bridge, he entered the vacant lot, high dry weeds poking to his chest. He felt strong and clear, the heroin running like chilled water through his body. Then he fell back on his ass as a pleasure-wave knocked him over.

"Do you have the toll?" A deep voice bellowed from above. Through the weeds, he could see an immense black man in a trench coat, pulled back to reveal a ripped Van Halen T-shirt covering a fat-rippled gut. He was wearing sweatpants tucked into cowboy boots, and for some reason, spurs.

"The toll?"

"For you, not much," the big man smiled. "You were very helpful handling Homeless Gary. Got my kingdom back." He spread his arms widely. "I would take just a touch of what's left in your little plastic bag. And later, maybe you can treat me to an Egg McMuffin." The shimmering form extended an arm. "I'm Balthazar," he said. "I've been waiting for you. My palace is just over there, under the bridge. The finest palace you've ever seen. Has a Samsung flat screen. There's room for you there."

Ian flailed for the man's arm which suddenly disappeared, and he fell backward. Balthazar was gone, but through the weeds, he could see the door to the palace, wedged into a corner below the bridge, right above the freeway.

Balthazar appeared again, standing just inside the entrance, motioning at Ian in with a happy smile. He pushed up on his cane and stumbled forward, anxious to finally come home.

A LETTER TO THE GOVERNOR

Dear Governor:

I'm penning this from the drafty confines of my ten-by-ten-foot cell, in the hope you can undo a great wrong. Governor, I'm an innocent man! I know most of letters you receive with a Texas Correctional system postmark probably make this claim, but in my case, the appeal is from a true victim of our fallible justice system. I was imprisoned by an incompetent prosecutor, intent on building his reputation at any cost, including sentencing an innocent man to death.

Perhaps worse than my own potential demise is the agony of confinement. You can't imagine the conditions I'm forced to endure. My hours are spent in a tiny box, walls the color of baby vomit. Pungent odors waft the hallways, and at night I sleep with Koss noise-cancelling head phones, to drown out the screams of the insane and brutally violated. Imagine being forced to defecate without privacy into a chilly stainless steel commode. Or even worse, having the deranged animal in the cell across from you in plain sight as he "does his business," all the while smiling and bellowing offensive Mexican ballads.

And the food! Would it break the State's budget to occasionally allow the incarcerated an heirloom tomato? Perhaps our prison population would be more manageable if we were given a thimble of Cabernet now and then to cleanse our pallets, or enough healthy fiber to clear our bowels of the putrid dreck that comprises prison cuisine. May I suggest a Mediterranean diet might improve our health and mindset?

But I'm off point. I trust you are aware of my alleged crime, but I fear you only know the tabloid version that the cartoonishly-evil district attorney, Mr. Preston Anderson, so successfully propagated. Here are the facts: My lovely wife, Ms. Mirabelle Hayes, was tragically killed in a whitewater rafting trip.

While it's true I was piloting the raft, I had nothing to do with her death. Certainly, I can't be held responsible for the herculean power of a class four river, nor my wife's adventurous spirit. Mr. Anderson, costumed in his jury-friendly seersucker suit, portrayed me as a sociopathic near-do-well; the kind of man that would marry a wealthy ninety-one-year-old woman, then take her into the wilds and cruelly cast her overboard for the sake of a twenty-million-dollar inheritance. This might make for an interesting Lifetime Movie of the Week, but is far from the truth.

While I acknowledge the considerable age gap between Mirabelle and myself, I hardly think less-than-conventional attractions warrant a death sentence. I know men that prefer their women young, perhaps hefty, or of a different creed or color. One of my fellow inmates claims a perverse attraction to paraplegics and dwarfs. Should I go to jail because I fell in love with a beautiful gal sixty years my senior? The heart wants what the heart wants. Would we put a teenager in jail because he fantasized about Dame Helen Mirren? Certainly not.

Be assured that the prosecutor's inference that I actually prefer the company of men is a complete fabrication. I agree with your position that God intended man to be with women, "Eve not Steve" being my credo. And while I'm a fan of their products, I'm not remotely acquainted with the effeminate Aldo's shoe salesman presented at the trial claiming to be my lover. He was clearly just another bad actor in Mr. Anderson's fictional production. Besides, a true footwear professional wouldn't come to court wearing Bass boat shoes.

The Prosecutor's assertion that Mirabelle was so senile she didn't know we were going rafting, and assumed I was taking her to Cinnabon, is ridiculous. My wife detested pastry and loved water, and was an accomplished swimmer. In fact, in 1935 she was runner-up in the 100-meter freestyle at the Texas State Swim Meet. My only regret is that I am not as powerful an aquanaut as she, or perhaps I could have come to her rescue.

I admit that due to overwhelming grief, my actions after her death were a bit unconventional, but Governor, I ask that you try to comprehend the fragile soul of an artist. As you might be aware, I am a writer of some acclaim, having published stories in publications that include Ellery Queen, and Southwest Airlines in-flight magazine. The story I optioned to HBO after Mirabelle's passing, Murder on the River, though inspired by my awful episode, was entirely fictional.

Like Fitzgerald, I express sadness via my prose. In retrospect I realize that crafting a tale about a young gay man that murders his elderly wife on a boating trip, then becomes famous by admitting the crime, could be misconstrued, but to be honest I was consumed by a broken heart, and the glamour of my new-found fame.

As an icon that has lived the limelight, you understand the power of national television. It was intoxicating to be in New York, squired between talk shows in shiny black sedans like Brad Pitt. I'm sorry, but a man with George Stephanopoulos's wily interrogatory skills could get a person to admit anything. I was dazzled by Good Morning America, selfishly wanting to hang-out and see Mumford and Sons play in the courtyard. Drunk with attention, and confused by George's insidious probing, I didn't intend to claim credit for my wife's murder. I assumed we were discussing my fictional story. You and I both know the press is an evil temptress.

So please, Governor, I throw myself on your mercy. Texas need not waste their precious Pentobarbital on an innocent man whose only crime was unconventional love, and a writing talent so vivid that fiction appears as fact. Use your deadly drugs on the truly guilty, like the awful man in the cell across from me. Do the courageous thing and set me free.

Yours in Christ,
Clifton DuMont Edwards, MFA

PUBLICATION CREDITS

Dick Cheney Shot Me in the Face first appeared in Talking River.

Fake Girlfriend first appeared in The Mississippi Review, and the anthology Theatre B.

One Star first appeared in Nivalis 2016.

The Tower first appeared in The Bookends Review.

Hecklers first appeared in 2 Bridges Review.

Regarding Your Ex-Wife first appeared in Fabula Argentea.

Impala first appeared in Heater, Abstract Jam, and the anthology *The Prison Compendium*.

The Purification first appeared in the anthology And All our Yesterdays.

Midnight Elvis first appeared in The Story Shack and The Eunoia Review.

Bouncing first appeared in the anthology Black Coffee.

Costco Girl first appeared in Mulberry Fork Review.

First Kill first appeared in Aestas 2015.

Everyone Loves Meatloaf first appeared in Fabula Argentea.

Adolph's Return first appeared in The Fredericksburg Literary Review.

A Letter to the Governor first appeared in Crack the Spine.

PUBLICATION CREDITS